Panther Shield

Guardians of Chaos 4

C.D. Gorri

Panther Shield
Guardians of Chaos Book 4
by C.D. Gorri
Edited by BookNookNuts
Copyright 2021 C.D. Gorri, NJ

*To the stoics, the quiet ones, the ones who keep us up at night, we
know what's going on inside your head, and we love it...*

*STOP! Before you go, sign up for my newsletter and get the latest
on my releases, giveaways, freebies and more:*
SUBSCRIBE HERE

Blurb

She's a fierce Panther Shifter fighting to preserve the freedom of all magic. He's a normal with a target on his back. Will she risk it all for him?

Elena Soussa is the only female Guardian of Chaos in her group. A Panther Shifter, she is a loner by nature, but ever since the members of her crew started meeting their mates and gaining new powers, her curiosity has been piqued.

When she finds a normal cornered by the enemy, she is compelled to save the ridiculously handsome man, but to do so means violating the Guardians' code.

He is not her problem, but her inner she-Cat sure wants him to be.

Will Elena risk it all for one man's life?

Guardians of Chaos Pledge

I am the watcher in the storm.
I am the iron shield.
I protect against those who seek to control the wild
nature of magic.
I am the guardian of chaos.
To thrive, we must be free.
From chaos comes creation.

Prologue

Elena grunted. She ducked the fierce blow coming from behind her.

Yes, her father was one hell of a fighter, but he'd taught his only daughter well. Too well. She'd been noticed for her antics at school, and on the varsity basketball team. One of the only females to reach six feet in height, she'd been a shoe in for the position as starting point guard since she'd been a freshman.

But this wasn't a basketball game. This was training with her dad, and Anthony Soussa took no prisoners. He was one tough SOB, and his little girl was a chip off the old block.

Elena fell into a defensive stance, gritting her teeth with the effort it took not to shift into her stealthy and more powerful Panther counterpart. That simply was not an option out in the streets where too many normals could witness such a supernatural feat.

That was why all the hand-to-hand combat training. She had to rely on her human body to get the job done. A Shifter was faster, stronger, and deadlier than any normal. Elena knew that by heart. But relying on her animal side could prove fatal, as it had for her late mother.

A police officer stationed in the rough city of Newark, New Jersey, Jasmine Soussa had been killed when a routine traffic stop turned deadly. The normals, group of hotheaded, low level drug dealers, had panicked and gunned down the female in broad daylight when Elena had been just four years old.

Unable to shift to her sleek Panther because of the number of humans in the area, Elena's mother had taken nine bullets to the chest and abdomen before succumbing to her injuries. It had been a horrible tragedy and had even made the papers. To this day Elena hated the sound of bagpipes and could still hear them playing in her head whenever she thought of that rainy Autumn morning when they'd buried her mother.

Jasmine's husband and Elena's father, Sergeant

Anthony Soussa, swore from that day on he would do everything in his power to see their only daughter grow up strong and fierce. But he'd accomplished much more than an increased sense of self-preservation in his child.

By the time Elena turned seventeen, she was the deadliest Panther in the small group of like Shifters that roamed the city of Newark. They were their own task force, and it was her dealings with thugs, supernatural and not, that got her noticed by one of the most elite forces in all of the supernatural world. The Guardians of Chaos.

She'd thought the legendary group of supernaturals was nothing more than a myth. The same thing went for Dragons and Vampires. That was, until she met one of each waiting for her after the brief high school graduation ceremony that had come and gone with no notice from her dad. Anthony Soussa had too much on his plate to worry about mundane human celebrations, so she'd been alone when they'd approached.

The Vampire had looked at her with impassive eyes, and the Diamond Dragon had merely sized her up. After their introduction, they'd explained who they were and what they wanted.

"You're unique, Elena, but your antics will get

you noticed by the normals, eventually. Let us put your substantial skills to better use. Help us defend magic. Help us keep it free for all beings. What do you say?" Byram, the Vampire, spoke first.

"Do I get to kick ass?"

"Fuck yeah," Kingston, the Dragon and Alpha of the group, replied.

"Then I'm in."

Elena had needed no time to think it over. She'd agreed to join them on the spot. Of course, she had yet to tell her father, and that was scary enough. Anthony Soussa swore his daughter would be tough, but he didn't want her anywhere near law enforcement, normal or not. And what were the Guardians if not supernatural cops?

He would never agree to it. Her father had already given too much to keep the people of the world safe, or so he always said. But this was her life and her choice. Elena stood up, accepting the bottle of water her father held out to her.

"Good match," he said, drinking from his own bottle. "But watch your reaction times, Elena. You seemed a bit off today."

"Dad? I have to talk to you," she called to him just as someone knocked on the front door.

"One moment," he replied, and turned to see who had come visiting their small

Shit.

They were early.

"Hello Mr. Soussa, we're here to collect Elena..."

And the rest was history.

Chapter One

"Elena, we've been through this," Egros turned to her, his eyes changing from blue to green to silver as his anger flared.

"I know, Eg, but there has to be something else you can give me to stop my stupid heat cycle!"

"You're just delaying the inevitable. You are a Panther Shifter, big cats go into heat once they reach adulthood. As you continue to deny yours, it will only get stronger and more frequent every time it comes upon you," he added.

The male Witch closed the alchemy book he'd been reading and slammed it on his desk. He'd been working with Jessenia, Furio's mate and a kitchen Witch, as well as Holley, another talented Witch mated to their group Alpha, on finding a way to stop the symptoms of Elena's heat cycle. But so far, nothing. The results of their inquiries and experiments were not good.

It always amazed her the rest of the supernatural world hadn't banded together, but most ignored the plights of their females. Pregnancy rates were notoriously low for supernaturals and there was no rush to deny what little chance they had at reproducing.

Regardless of how unfair it was to the females involved. Elena growled angrily. She was no one's fucking handmaiden. And she would not be forced to copulate and reproduce. It was barbaric!

Holley had concocted a potion made of several wild herbs she'd found growing near the Keep, and so far, so good, but the effects were wearing off at an alarming rate. Instead of her heat hitting her once a quarter, it was more like every month for the past year. Looked like Egos' grim predictions were right.

Fury flooded her system, threatening to force a shift, but Elena was in control. Always. She reined in her inner kitty, pushed the snarling she-Cat back, and counted to three before meeting Egros' curious stare.

This simply was not fair. She was a warrior, a fierce Panther Shifter, a true Guardian of Chaos. They were neck deep in this war with the Loyalists, and she did not have time for this shit. Elena had been training for this her entire life.

Hadn't she left her father and her home before she'd turned eighteen for this reason? To protect the world of magic at all costs. She was not cut out to be a mother. Hell, she didn't even have a prospect, much less a mate. Regardless of what tradition dictated, she wasn't getting knocked up by some stranger simply to preserve the species. Fuck that.

Elena had too much self-respect to be a damn incubator. If and when she had a cub, it would be on her terms. Not some biological imperative. Anger coursed through her, and she kicked at something on the floor, sending the box of whatever flying across the room.

"Hey! Those are my files, thank you very much," grumbled Egros.

"Sorry. Ugh," she moaned and sat down on a stool while he checked the data log on his computer.

While she waited, memories of her own mother crowded her brain. She recalled the sweet way she used to brush Elena's pale blonde hair and tie the laces on her patent leather shoes. Elena had loved her strong, fierce mother, especially all the attention the female gave to her only daughter.

As a child, she had been ultrafeminine. Pink was

her favorite color. She'd played dolls and pretended to be a mother with her own brood of beautiful babies. It was something she'd envisioned from a very young age, being a mother and having a mate, a family of her own.

The sudden violent death of her mother had put a stop to that kind of innocent daydreaming. Elena's warm and once happy home had instantly turned into a training dojo, and her once carefree father had become her brutally honest instructor.

It was a difficult change for a teenage girl, but she'd learned to cope. More than that. Elena had excelled at combat. She had a real feel for it and had spent years training, perfecting the skill set coveted by organizations such as the Guardians.

She'd been approached by the usual normal agencies, CIA, FBI, and a few black ops mercenary groups. But Elena was not interested in the petty wars of humankind.

She was a Shifter, and her place was serving the supernatural world. Kingston Baldric, the Alpha of their group of Guardians, had offered her the job, and she'd never looked back.

Where else could she use all of her power, speed, and the fierceness of her Panther to get the job accomplished? The Guardians of Chaos were more than her employers, they were her family. But this business with her heat was getting in the way.

What started out as a way for her father to work out his grief and protect his daughter had turned into a way of life for the she-Cat. Elena had truly learned to love the deadly beauty and grace that accompanied her many mixed martial arts trainings.

She was an expert with several black belts in varying degrees, having studied combat with masters the world over. Neela, the late wife of their leader and Alpha, Kingston Baldric, was one of her mentors.

It had been difficult for Elena to accept Holley as his mate, but after she'd learned the circumstances of his first mating to Neela, the Panther Shifter understood and respected her Alpha even more. The complicated relationship he'd endured with the she-Dragon bespoke of a man of real honor and worth.

Holley was lucky to have him. Hell, he was lucky to have her, too. In fact, it seemed as if more and more of their group of Guardians were finding their mates these days. Pregnancies were running rampant too, with Holley nearly ready to give birth and Fergie announcing her own coming pups just the other day.

Elena was overjoyed for them, and yet, she felt sadness and grief, some guilt as well. She knew nothing like that would never happen for her. The Fates had not aligned to grant her a mate. Besides, she knew she was far from ready for cubs of her own.

Imagine finding her own Fated mate? Ha! That was only a dream for someone like her. Which is why the whole thing with her heat cycle was especially cruel.

Shifter males preferred human females, or even Witches, as they were nearly human. Shifter females, rare and precious, were typically coddled by whatever Pack, Clan, or Pride they belonged too. Elena had been none of those things.

Panthers were lone creatures, existing in smallish family groups, but no real Prides. She had no affiliations with any other group than the Guardians. Just the fact she'd chosen to hone her warrior's skills instead of finding someone suitable to impregnate her was enough to tell all males for miles and miles exactly where her priorities laid.

It was not with a potential mate or family. It was with the Guardians. She had no one else, and that was okay with her.

Keep telling yourself that.

Shut up!

Elena snarled at the snarky bitch inside her head. Her inner kitty was getting rather nasty lately. The beast was antsy and restless. Just other ways to say horny, she scoffed derisively. Then Elena clutched her stomach as a wave of pain almost sent her crashing to the floor.

"Elena!" Egros rushed over and took her hand, but she pushed him aside, not wanting his touch.

In fact, her Panther hissed and growled. She was not having any of that Witch. He was a friend, but nothing more. Not now or ever.

"I'll be fine."

"You're not fine. Your heat is coming back already!"

"So, what? I'm supposed to stop being a Guardian, now? I'm just supposed to stay home barefoot and pregnant cause fucking biology? Bull shit," she snarled.

"Here. Try this, but I warn you it will not stop it," Egros said, ignoring her bad temper. He handed her a vial.

"This is the last of Holley's potion, but at the rate you are metabolizing the herbs, it will wear off within a few hours."

"Thanks," she growled. Tossing back the bitter tasting shot of potion with a hiss of displeasure.

"I could always, you know, *help*."

Egros' voice was so low she almost missed it, but

Elena was a Shifter with supernaturally enhanced hearing. The fact she could sense his lust made her beast growl angrily. The she-Cat would not have him. She wouldn't even think about letting him touch her.

Odd. Her reaction was so strong, but Elena thought about his offer, or at least pretended to. She shook her head. For a while now, she'd suspected the male Witch of having some sort of crush on her. But the cold hard truth of it was Elena did not reciprocate his feelings.to

"No," she replied, and shook her head. "That would not be wise, Egros, and you know it."

"I know, El. But I mean, you need me, and I am here. I can't bear to think of you in pain---"

"No. I will be fine."

Elena walked out of the new potions room the Keep had magically whipped up for the now three resident witches and turned down the ever changing hallway. She shook her head, mindful of her destination, and walked until she stood before her door.

"Shit," she whispered, and walked into her sitting room.

Each Guardian had their own suite of rooms in the Keep, and hers was perhaps the largest aside from Kingston's, simply because she had been there the longest after Storm. Elena had been a Guardian almost fifty years now.

Shifters aged differently than normals, sometimes hardly if at all. Guardians were granted longevity in return for their dedication and service to all species, and, of course, magic itself. In all that time, she had eluded her heat cycle successfully. She closed her eyes and sunk down on the plush purple couch. The color was dark, almost black, and fabulously soft.

Despite being a rough and tumble warrior, Elena had to admit she liked her creature comforts. Sure, there was also a barre against one wall that she used for stretches and to strengthen her core and tonality. An old wing chun wooden dummy occupied one corner, and a ten-foot cat scratching post the other.

She really had to replace that thing, she thought with a frown. Her inner kitty sure did love keeping her claws nice and sharp. Elena rolled her shoulders and closed her eyes.

She only had precious few hours until the potion wore off, then her feline would be yowling and prowling for a male to sate her biological imperative to mate. Not to find her actual mate. Just mate. As in fuck.

Sigh.

Feeling all sorts of gnarly, she stood up and tore off her clothing, opting for a quick shift and stretch in the warm rays of sunshine filtering through the enormous oval skylight before she had to do what needed to be done.

Elena welcomed the magic that transformed her nearly six feet of powerful woman to a sleek black Panther nearly triple her human weight. She didn't know how the Keep did it since the outside resembled a medieval castle, but she was grateful all the same.

Her inner kitty simply loved the sunshine. The idea of what she was about to do was both intriguing and somewhat nerve racking. She'd never been the type of woman who indulged in one night stands.

But she couldn't fight what was essentially her biological makeup. Elena was an unmated feline Shifter of the age to bear cubs, and her Panther was fully aware of that.

Kitty cat wanted a cub, whether she'd found her mate or not was irrelevant. And if she couldn't have that, she damn sure wanted to practice making one.

Fuck me. Elena thought, whipping her sleek tail back and forth while stretching in the sunshine.

Yes, please. Her feline pushed back at her.

Looked like she was going to need a few minutes

with Fergie, Holley, and Jessenia before she went out. The three females were mated to Elena's fellow Guardians and were as close to gal pals as she'd ever had.

They were pretty damn awesome. And Elena needed some advice. But first, she could take a little fortifying catnap, couldn't she?

Prrrrr.

Chapter Two

*D**ammit.*

Logan slammed his hands on the stainless steel worktable of his makeshift lab. Having his own money came in handy when he'd left his cozy job with big pharma and decided to dive into his research on his own.

Logan Wells had been on the verge of a groundbreaking discovery when his own bosses had shut him down. He didn't need them. He had connections, wealth, and more degrees than he could count. But that would not help him now.

The sample was contaminated. It was the only thing that made sense.

Human cells did not regenerate at such an aggressive rate, nor with such fantastic results. If they could, minor injuries would require no attention. And what was thought of as major injuries, like those received in a motor vehicle accident, would be gone with nothing more than an aspirin, and a pat on the head.

No. Something was wrong. The blood sample he'd personally taken from the victim of the warehouse explosion, who'd still been miraculously alive when responders had attended the scene, up until about twenty minutes ago, could not be untainted.

When Logan had seen footage of the aftermath of the explosion downtown, he'd sincerely doubted there were any survivors. But the EMTs and hospital ER docs had assured him, the patient had come from the wreckage, and he'd survived all of two days with 99% of his body covered in burns, and broken bones and torn ligaments from the weight of the debris on his body.

The old, supposedly empty building had been devastated by the explosion. Some suspected terrorists or secret arms dealers testing their wares of being behind the blast. Terrible, but not his purview.

His sister would smack him upside the head for that callous thought, but Margo wasn't there and, far as he knew, his twin couldn't read his mind even if she were.

Twin. Ha ha.

He smirked, thinking about his sister. The female had brass balls the size of boulders. She was tough as they came, and he couldn't have been more proud of her.

Of course, Grandfather always hated when he'd called his father's bastard his twin. But it had nothing to do with the later patriarch of the Wells family.

Margo Sinclair Wells was born on the same day as Logan, just minutes apart, in the same hospital even. Must have been convenient for his dad to walk from one room holding his first born son and heir, down the hall to see his newborn daughter from a longstanding affair. Logan's mother was crushed by her husband's infidelity, but she stayed with him till the tragic end, and made damn sure he got to know his sister.

As far as Logan was concerned, he and Margo shared fathers, were born on the same day, and had ever since developed a long standing bond that was rare between siblings far as he could tell. She was his twin. Even if he was as pasty as his English ancestors, and she dark as her African ones. Twins. And fuck what anyone else thought.

Margo shared the same high intellect with her

brother, and he'd often suspected her of having an eidetic memory. Not that she spoke of it. She'd thrown herself into law and fought hard to right the injustices that plagued the judicial system.

A bleeding heart, he'd often joked. But his sister was the youngest black female attorney to be courted for judgeship. She'd turned it down for a stint in the FBI, and as he understood from her last email, she was elbows deep in some European shit hole hunting down one of the masterminds on their most wanted list.

Margo was tough as nails, but she always cared about the people involved in a crime while Logan spent his time finding other ways to benefit humanity. Like with his research. The warehouse explosion was terrible, but useful, too. Or it would have been, had his sample not been fucked.

Dammit.

It wasn't that Logan did not care about heinous acts of violence symbolic of a depraved mind or grossly desensitized individual. More so that as a geneticist and biochemist on the edge of a breakthrough in his research that could possibly alleviate real human ailments that have plagued humankind for centuries, he simply did not have the time to care about hunting down criminals.

To his way of thinking, there were people born to certain jobs. Everyone had their place in the universe, and some were lucky enough to know what their place was. Like him. He was a scientist and someday his work could cure things like dementia, arthritis, high blood pressure, diabetes, and more. Wouldn't that be amazing?

Hell. He had the skill set. Logan had been courted by world renowned hospitals and big pharma, but after his first stint with a famous drug company, he'd learned his lesson.

That very first job, he'd been so young and bright eyed, eager to make a difference. Logan had discovered a way to tap into a person's bio-chemical makeup to help regulate one's need for medicine. His research was bought, sealed, and then locked away for good.

Defeated and forced to sign an NDA, Logan left the company and had been using his trust fund to live and to pay for his own experiments. Someday, he could help humankind. That was the promise he'd made to his grandfather, whom he was named after, on the man's deathbed. And it was the promise he'd made himself after he packed his desk and walked out on that old job.

He still remembered the impression Logan Wells

I had made on him, an orphaned boy of just six, when he'd gone to live with the man. It was as if the giant silver haired version of the adult Logan would become had looked right into his soul.

"You'll do alright, lad. Aye, you will."

But was he really? Logan couldn't help but feel like a total fucking failure. He was thirty-five years old. No wife. No kids. No job. He had his research, but no one would touch him after he'd sued his former bosses. Life was pretty much screwed for him.

His cell went off and he looked down. Shit. He was late for his set.

"Fuck. Fuck. FUCK!" he growled and slammed the desk again.

Temper, temper, his grandfather would have said, but fuck it. Logan had grown up on the streets of Newark, money or not. He was a foul mouthed genius, and he knew it.

"It's fucking contaminated," he grumbled as he hauled ass out of the makeshift lab he'd assembled in the basement of his townhouse.

He didn't care for opulence. He cared for privacy. Owning his own townhouse gave him just enough. Logan grabbed the case holding his *Rickenbacker Fireglo* and ran to catch his Uber.

Playing bass at *Midnight's* on Thursdays was just one of Logan's creative outlets. Even science nerds needed to blow off steam now and then. Like most teens, he used that period of angst in his life to study music, try his hand at the whole garage band thing.

Unfortunately, at the time, rock and blues were out of style, and boy bands were all the rage. He and his pals had no chance of getting anywhere. So, he'd turned to more scientifical pursuits, thinking that road would be rewarding. Unfortunately, disappointment abounded.

"You're late," Rick Melon, the bouncer, stated as Logan passed him on his way to the stage.

It was a small night spot in downtown Newark, four blocks away from Newark Penn Station and across the street from a *Dinosaur Barbecue*. The *Prudential Center* where the New Jersey Devils hockey team played was another city block over.

Not the ideal spot for a rock bar, but *Midnight's* did surprisingly well. Logan barely noticed the snow on the ground as he ran from the Uber driver's nondescript sedan to the back door of the establishment.

He grabbed his glass of iced tea from Simone, one of the bartenders, and got on stage standing off to the side and between Elliot, the front man, who glared at him, Denise, ignored him as usual while she fiddled with her guitar, and Roger, the drummer, simply tipped his head. After another second, Elliot got over his pissy mood, and they started to play.

Logan was unsure how many hours had passed while he poured his frustration into his music. He did, however, note the moment she walked in.

Holy fuck.

He'd seen beautiful women before. Plenty of them. Logan was rich, smart, not bad looking, and he played bass. Getting women had never been difficult for him. Especially not at that time in his life, when getting women to fill his bed was all that mattered.

She was different, though. Something about her had every eye, male and female alike, zeroed in on the miles of ivory skin revealed in the skimpy miniskirt and tank top. February in New Jersey meant snow and temperatures in the single digits, but this woman had no coat, no hat, no scarf. Just two scraps of fabric that barely covered her tight assets.

Wouldn't they look great on my floor?

He missed a note, staring as hard as he was, it was a wonder he didn't face plant right off the fucking stage. The lights were dark, but even in the glow of the dark blue lights, Logan could tell something was different about the female.

She looked to be casing the joint. Not to rob it. But for something. He licked his lips, keeping time with the song, but no longer feeling it as he watched her scanning for something. He didn't know why it interested him. Was uncertain why he should care what the pretty woman was looking for, but he did. A lot.

In fact, he held his breath until she stopped searching. His lungs burned with the need for oxygen, but Logan couldn't fucking move. It was like she'd cast some sort of spell on him. The song ended, thank fuck, and Elliot announced their break.

Good thing too. Logan had stopped playing a few bars before the song had finished. Elliot was next to him, chewing him out between gritted teeth, but Logan could not give two shits what the jerk was talking about.

Then her eyes landed on him, and suddenly, he could breathe again. He gulped in air greedily, watching, star struck, as she walked over to him. All grace and lithe, like a ballet, she glided across the dark room until she was standing right there. At the foot of the stage.

He did not want to blink, refused to miss even a

moment of watching the gorgeous creature. The lighting was bad, the room too crowded, and fuck, he wasn't sure, but he thought her eyes were the color of bubble gum. Dark pink, otherworldly, and so fucking hot.

Logan swallowed. He ignored the approach of one of Midnight's regulars. A fellow scientist, the squat little man, chatted him up occasionally. He was older, used to work for some big pharma label. He was there every Thursday and smelled like beer and stale pretzels. A harmless guy, but Logan was suddenly furious with him for trying to snag his attention.

"Hey Dr. Wells, missed a few notes tonight, huh? You know I've been meaning to talk to you about your research---"

"Not now, Harry," he growled, actually fucking growled at the guy.

What the hell was wrong with him? Logan was neither aggressive nor rude, but right then, he was both. The female smirked, pink eyes flashing at him while she slinked her way across the dance floor.

She moved like a predator on the prowl with a singular focus that he thanked fuck seemed to be him. Logan had never experienced such a thrilling surge of desire for a woman, but his reaction was unmistakable. His cock ached, rock hard against the suddenly too abrasive material of his briefs and jeans.

He wanted the stranger. Could picture himself now buried to the hilt in her slick heat, or with his head between her long legs, licking her to ecstasy. Fuck him. When did he ever want that? To taste a woman so damn badly he was salivating for her?

Never, that was when. Never had Logan ever wanted to drop to his knees and eat some pretty woman's pussy until she was panting for him, screaming his name, pulling his hair. Fuck yes. He pictured all that in the span of time it took to blink.

And she knew it. Somehow, he knew she could tell how much he wanted her. It was in the naughty sparkle in her incredible eyes, and the way her fair hair sparkled like silver starlight in the shitty blue lighting from the bar. It was in every single step she took in that too short skirt, and those killer fuck me boots.

"But Wells, I really think we should tal---"

Logan pushed Harry's hand off his shoulder, moving closer to the woman as she stepped directly into his space.

"Meet me in the alley in three minutes."

Her husky voice stroked along his skin like hands

roaming his body, and damn it, he really wanted that. Her hands on his skin. Like now. She waited, he realized for an answer and found himself unable to speak. That kind of proposal was completely out of character for a guy like him, and yet, Logan found himself nodding his agreement.

The gorgeous woman grinned, biting her lower lip, she eyed him from head to toe like he was a tasty meal, and she couldn't wait to dive in. Fuck, he couldn't either. Then she turned to leave out the front, and he was pushing past poor Harry, grabbing the case for his bass, and putting away the thing while shrugging into his jacket.

"Hey man, we have another set!" Elliot yelled, but Logan ignored the band's front man and took off for the back door like a man possessed.

Squinting against the darkness, he ignored the cold, the sight of breath like smoke streaming from his nose and mouth, and scanned the dank alleyway for the woman. A sleek sports car pulled up and the passenger door opened.

"Well?" Her husky voice reached him, and Logan didn't think he just acted.

Another first for the usually careful scientist. He jumped into the car and slammed the door behind him. The woman grabbed him by his shirt and slammed her mouth to his.

"Address?" she asked on a whimper, and he rambled off his address to her, not thinking or even caring if she was going to rob him, beat him, whatever, as long as she kept kissing him.

And she did. Eyes on the road, she damn near pulled all six and a half feet of him across her lap while her tongue stroked his as she zipped in and out of traffic.

Logan was so fucking turned on he couldn't think straight. Eyes like bubble gum, he realized that was what she tasted like too. Sweet like candy, but more than that. She was deep, refined, like a good bottle of wine, and he was so fucking thirsty.

She purred against him, and he licked his way to her neck and chest, tugging the skimpy material aside so he could suck one pert nipple into his mouth. His dick was so hard he almost came from the thrill alone.

Then she was pulling into a spot and throwing the sleek little vehicle into park. Logan moaned as she pulled his head up, forcing him to release her breast.

"Keys?" she asked, panting with need.

"Yeah," he said, reaching into his back pocket and handing them to her.

Then they were both groping and kissing each other as they moved up his stairs to his townhouse. Finally, they opened the door. He didn't care about finding the bed or couch. Hell, he couldn't think about anything other than touching her.

She pulled her top off, then went to work on his while he buried his head between her breasts. Her skin was white as alabaster, smooth and soft, and he couldn't get enough of it.

His hands inched downwards, finding her thighs in the tight little skirt. He crept under it, moaning again when he found she was bare beneath the tiny little bit of fabric.

"Fuck, that feels so good," she moaned, tossing her head back as he picked her up and pressed her against the wall.

Logan dropped to his knees, prepared to do anything for the beautiful goddess. He kissed her inner thighs, loving the tight pull of her fingers on his hair. Then he was there, kissing, licking, and sucking her tight little nubbin, relishing in the heat of her wet folds.

"You taste so good," he growled, pressing his tongue inside her.

The woman hissed and growled, a real wildcat, she pulled his hair until he had to look up.

"Ouch. What is it?"

"Need you in me. Now," she growled, and his dick went even harder.

Fumbling for a condom, he sheathed himself before pressing into her right there against the wall. There was no stopping the avalanche of feeling that damn near consumed him as he fucked the gorgeous creature against his living room wall. Muscles bunched, she wrapped her long legs around his hips, skirt bunched around her waist, nails scratching at his shoulders, and Logan pumped his hips furiously.

"Yes, fuck, yes," she groaned, head tossed back, pink eyes wide as he pistoned faster and harder.

Sweat droplets coated his brow and ecstasy teased his nerve endings, it was just there, so close so close. But he never was a selfish lover, and more than anything, he wanted to feel this woman come on his rigid cock, wanted to revel in every squeeze and flutter of her perfect pussy.

"Need," she moaned, squeezing him tighter.

"I have what you need," he growled the words in a mostly testosterone fueled reply.

Then he was reached between them, strumming her tight little nubbin, playing with her clit as his cock stroked along her walls. And then she was coming.

"Oh gods!" the beautiful stranger screamed, her walls gripping him so hard, he went cross-eyed for a moment, pumping two, three, four more times before chasing her right off the edge into untold bliss.

A couple of hours and three condoms later, Logan lay in a spent heap on the rug in front of the fireplace. The beautiful blonde woman curled into his side, dozing lightly after their sex marathon, not that he could blame her. He was tired too.

Deliciously exhausted, and totally, completely sated. Really, that was a first. He'd read about passion like he'd just experienced. The kind that burned bright like wildfire or supernovas.

Poets wrote about it, musicians paid homage to it in song and artists created paintings and sculptures, but he never expected to find it at *Midnight's*. And he didn't even know her name.

In the morning, he told himself. He'd ask her in the morning. Then he draped an arm across her stomach and spooned in close, ignoring his hard on in favor of sleep. The woman with the pink eyes sighed and snuggled closer, and Logan drifted off easily for the first time in years.

Chapter Three

What the hell?

Elena blinked awake suddenly. Where the hell was she? The room was immaculate. Like cleaning crew clean. Expensive furniture straight out of a catalog. As if the person who lived there had money but not a lot of time.

Made sense. She wasn't much of an interior decorator either, preferring comfort to label. Elena sat up and the person beside her snored, shifting slightly in his sleep.

Uh oh.

Suddenly, the events leading up to her waking in that strange place came flooding back, and with alarming clarity. Sated and unalarmed, her inner kitty purred as she gazed down at the human male she'd chosen earlier that night to see her through her heat.

Her first thought was that the strange man was just so pretty. Not effeminate, just beautiful. He mumbled something in his sleep, and she stilled, not wanting to wake him.

Okay.

So, what she really wanted was to avoid him altogether. Nothing more awkward than being caught sneaking out after doing the dirty. Guilt assailed her, but she pushed it away.

She had no cause for that now. There was nothing nefarious about this. Just some no-strings sex between consenting adults. Her she-Cat snarled, and pushed her to stay beside the sleeping male, but Elena shook it off.

Grrr.

She winced as she stood up, deliciously sore in places that had been neglected far too long. Her body missed the warmth from his the second she pulled away. He'd been so very big and tall, warm too.

She mourned the loss of his heat as she inched away from the little nest they'd made. He'd used a throw blanket and pillows from the nearby sofa to wrap around them as they'd spread out on the thick rug in front of the roaring fireplace.

Damn.

She'd had no intention of doing more than sating her heat and speeding away from the stranger. But the second he'd touched her, that notion had flown right out the window. Something had happened to Elena. Something that was beyond her control.

Mine.

Her inner kitty purred, pushing the thought into her head just as Elena caught herself almost brushing the dark hair that had spilled across his forehead away from his handsome face.

Shit.

She shrank back. Okay. Reality check. The man was cute. That much was true. But no way was he *hers*. Not in the sense her inner kitty meant.

Mate.

No.

Grrr.

Her Black Panther snarled angrily, but Elena ignored the frisky feline as she tugged on her top and skirt, ignoring the ridiculously high-heeled boots, then slipped outside. It was snowing, but she did not care a fig for the cold. She just had to get out of there, and fast.

She took the magical shortcuts the Guardians used to cross the distance between their home base and Newark in a fraction of the time. Normally, that was for emergencies only, but she was feeling all shook up and out of sorts.

Back at the Keep, Elena straightened her shoulders and walked in through the side door by the kitchen. Holley and Jessenia's kitchen garden was snowed over, but she noticed lights on in the greenhouse. The resident Witches used it to grow special herbs for potions and cooking year round.

Hopefully, whoever was in there stayed in there. She didn't want questions about where she'd spent the last few hours. Elena was keenly aware she stank of sex and man, but she was reluctant to jump in the shower just yet.

Truth was, she liked his scent. That mix of rain, spice, and man sent tendrils of remembered passion spiraling through her core. Every look, every touch, every meeting of lips had been beyond her scope of experience.

She was no virgin, but she'd never been as sexually active as others of her kind. It was completely natural, all physical, but she admittedly had issues with control. As in, she needed to be the one in control.

It irked her that she was at the mercy of her heat cycle. Actually, pissed her off was more like it. It was a curse, and yet, had she not been desperate for an outlet, she might not have met him. The tall, beautiful musician who lived in a townhouse seemed to have some money, kissed like a god, and rocked her world well into the wee hours of the morning. Far longer than she'd ever imagined any human capable.

That was all she knew about him. And it was going to have to be enough.

Mine.

No.

Yesss.

She rolled her eyes and closed the door soundlessly behind her. This was not the first time she'd used a male to see her through her heat.

Her previous partners were always supes like her, not human, but Jessenia, Fergie, and Holley had all assured her this kind of hook up was acceptable in normal society.

Still, she felt strange leaving him like that. Her past partners had known the deal beforehand. They understood she was at the mercy of her hormones and knew there would be no ties. Of course, this heat cycle had snuck up on her, and she'd had no time to make that kind of arrangement.

Egros had offered to partner with her, but she knew the Witch was not altogether honest about his motives. Her fellow Guardian seemed to be hiding some feelings for Elena.

Guilt and remorse struck a chord within her, but she shook it off. Whatever crush the male had developed on her, it was not her responsibility. She in no way encouraged him, and he needed to get over it. The faster the better.

The cold, hard truth was, she simply did not feel the same. Now, if it were a tall handsome normal with stunning hazel eyes and just the right amount of shadow on his cheeks, then she might be inclined to reevaluate her feelings.

Dammit. She really should not be having those thoughts. Why, oh why, had she listened to Fergie and Jessenia's advice? She shook her head, replaying the women's comments in her ear.

"Humans have one night stands all the time," the kitchen Witch had said.

"This way you'll be in total control," Fergie added. *"Find someone cute, boink his brains out. Or better yet, make sure he boinks your brains out. Then come back home. Easy peasy,"* the redhead stated *baldly.*

Yeah. Real fucking easy, she thought with a

frown. Her damn kitty thought the guy was her mate, and now the beast would not stop yowling and scratching at her insides. The pain of her heat cycle finally abated for now, but her she-Cat was positively furious at her.

"I can smell him on you."

Elena refused to jump or react in any way to Egros' voice, though it did catch her off guard. She turned slightly to see the Witch sitting at the counter, in the dark.

"It is none of your business, Eg," she replied.

Tension spiked between the two old friends, but Elena was so not going there with him. They were colleagues first, peers. He should respect her enough to know the limits of their relationship. More than that, she'd thought they were friends.

"A human? You went to a human over me?" His anger and hurt batted up against her like fists, and she stepped back in shock before holding her ground.

"Egros," Elena began, friendly yet firm. "Why would you say this to me? It has nothing to do with you. You are my friend and my colleague, but my personal life is not your business."

"And how can you say that to me," he asked, pointing at his chest. "I've tried my best to help you. I have been patient, waiting for you to notice me, but you chose a human? How could you do that to me?"

"What? It isn't about you at all! That's it, move out of my way, Egros. I am not discussing this with you anymore," she growled, shoving her way past him.

"I care for you, Elena---"

"Stop. Please, just stop."

The male Witch frowned hard, lines creasing his forehead and around his mouth. He was hurt. She scented it, felt it even, and that saddened her. But she was not about to explain to him or anyone else what she decided to do with her body. It was not his business.

"Fine. Do what you like, Elena," he replied, and shoved off the wall, preparing to leave.

Shoulders slumped, she headed towards her room. *Dammit.* This was not going how she'd planned at all. With her heat eased, she planned to get right back into the swing of her work as a Guardian. And yet, here she was, confused and missing a man whose name she did not know, and managing to piss off one of her dearest friends.

Sad yowl.

Chapter Four

The days passed one by one, a long succession of the same old for an entire week. Day in and day out, she'd trained, fought bad guys, and came home bruised, but sound.

Elena should have rejoiced in the steady success that was her sworn duty as a Guardian, but she felt off. As if she were missing a huge chunk of herself. All was right with the world, but something was bugging her.

Try as she might to hide it, the others could tell. Her fellow Guardians gave her a wide berth. Egros especially. Her relationship with the male Witch was tense as ever, but they were able to work still, and that should have pleased her. But needless to say, it didn't.

It wasn't until a very pregnant Holley grabbed her hand and pulled her towards the private room the Keep had designated just for the females in the house that Elena knew she could not deny her feelings anymore.

"Holley? What are you doing?"

"Shh, just wait," the little Witch growled as she passed her curious mate and some of the other males who were discussing tactics in the conference room.

Once they'd rounded the corner, a marvelous mahogany door emblazoned with the words *ladies only* in a glittering, scrawling script waited for them/ The door opened of its own accord, as it sometimes did by the spirits of the Keep.

Holley pulled Elena inside, something the Panther allowed for two reasons. One, the female was mated to their Alpha, whom she respected, and two, she held the tiny Witch in great esteem.

"Okay," Holley said, and turned to face her.

"What?"

"Now, I have had enough of that expression and your silence. Tell me, what is going on, El?" Holley asked, brows furrowed as she rubbed her small hands over her ever growing belly.

"Is it obvious?" Elena whispered, closing her

eyes, and sitting down heavily on one of the plush chairs.

"Yes. It is."

The door opened and Jessenia and Fergie filed in soon after. Both women took seats on the matching velvet chaise lounges the Keep had furnished for them.

The *Ladies' Room* was not a bathroom, despite the odd name. It was more like a replica of an enormous old-fashioned dressing room. The kind designed for boutiques in the 1950s equipped with a raised stage, excellent track lighting, with several full-length mirrors, and a running soundtrack that seemed to only play the *Rat Pack*.

It was done in pinks and golds. Completely girly, over the top frilly, and just plain lovely, it was the only place Elena indulged in her secret fascination with fashion. Everyone always expected her to be the consummate warrior. And she was fine with that for the most part, but Elena had other interests too.

Like the three females who sat now waiting for her to open up to them. It was strange and nice, actually. Elena never had girlfriends, but here she was with three of the best females she knew.

Fergie, a former normal turned Wolf by her mate

with an extravagant obsession with shoes, Holley a Witch who'd been trapped by a madman and rescued by her fated mate who was also a total clotheshorse, and Jessenia, the tiny kitchen Witch who stole the heart of their resident Italian Stallion.

They were the best friends she'd ever had, but there was so much unsaid. Things they could not possibly understand. Loneliness was portable, she supposed. Even in crowds.

Sighing, she raised her head and glanced around. This morose behavior had to stop. After all, these three women were waiting for her, not pushing her to confide in them. Maybe she was wrong about them not understanding.

Elena sighed as her eyes fell on a rack of clothes, she couldn't help but appreciate. They were just her speed. Tight pants, crop tops, the perfect fabric for battle or to hang around in. The Keep was learning her style and providing thusly. Not easy since at six feet of lean muscle, she was difficult to outfit.

Fergie always grumbled about her skinny ass, but it was just one of the perks of being a Panther. The gods knew she ate like a horse. *No offence, Furio,* she thought with a wicked grin as she picked a salmon canape off the tray Jessenia had brought in.

"Okay. I'll spill, but first, food. These are so good," she moaned in appreciation, and Jessenia practically glowed at the compliment.

"Wait till you try my peanut butter dream cookies for dessert!"

"OMG! Jess, what the hell are you tryin' to do to me? I'm already big as a house with this little cub growing inside me," Fergie fake-complained while munching on a canape in one hand and a cookie in the other.

"Well, my young dragonling and I are very pleased with your efforts," Holley said smiling around a cookie she'd snagged from the still covered dessert tray.

"You guys! Those are for after the canapes," Jess scolded. "And Fergie, you are not big as a house."

Jess paused, looked her BFF over, then opened her mouth again.

"Well, maybe your ass is a little bit bigger," she added.

"Oh yeah? Wait till that pony you keep riding knocks you up! We'll see whose ass is big then, heifer!" Fergie said, sticking her tongue out at her bestie.

"Dog breath!"

"Witch!"

After they'd exhausted their insults, both females burst out laughing. Holley rolled her eyes over the females' antics, gesturing to Elena that the two of them were nuts.

"Hey, did you ladies see what the Keep brought us?" Fergie giggled, wiping her mouth with a napkin, her fake fight with Jessenia already forgotten.

"Oh yeah, I so need this," Elena said, her pink gaze roaming over the latest gowns and baubles the Keep had magically created.

"Hey, how do we know this stuff isn't stolen?" Fergie asked for the millionth time.

"Because that is not how the *manetuwak* work," Holley repeated.

It was the same reply she always gave her. Elena had worried at first too that magical thievery was the means by which the Keep was getting their wares. She couldn't help but admire the racks and racks of delightful goods, but refused to wear them until Holley explained they were mostly replicas from famous designer labels.

Magically whipped up to suit their whims. If any of the ladies could think it, the Keep could make it. Besides, that was how Elena had found herself in the skimpy little outfit she'd worn the night her heat cycle had forced her out on the prowl.

"Alright, now before these two started going at it, Elena, I'd asked you a question," Holley spoke up.

"Oh? You did?"

"Yes, I did. Now, don't you think it's time you told us what's the matter?"

Holley's eyes narrowed in concern. She rubbed her belly and waited patiently for Elena to answer. No one was more patient and inspired more confidence than Holley, but she was unsure how to proceed.

"Nothing," she replied, figuring she might as well try ignoring her current dilemma.

"I know you're our resident badass, but please, we are friends here and this is the *Ladies' Room*! It's our safe haven, El," Holley said, obviously not taking the hint.

"She's right. Talk to us," Fergie seconded with her mouth full, so it sounded more like *she's wight twalk two ush.*

"OMG. Swallow first, Fergie," Jess said, then snorted. "Bet you hear that a lot from Storm, eh?"

"Okay, easy," Elena began, wanting to break up the friendly spat before it got out of hand. Fergie had that look in her eye, the same one she'd had when she hid one of every pair of shoes Jessenia owned.

Sigh. She really had a serious shoe fetish. But all kidding aside, what could Elena say?

Oh, I'm just mooning over some one night stand who probably forgot about me the second he woke up.

Not very badass of her. In fact, she was so shocked by her own reactions, she had no idea what to say.

"It's nothing," Elena began, deciding to spare her friends her own idiocy.

"That's it, I call bullshit," Fergie said not bothering to look up from the bowl of Jessenia's homemade mint cookie crunch ice cream she was currently munching on.

"Where did you get that ice cream? I hid that in the back of the freezer for Furio!"

"Yeah, well, finders keepers, beyotch," she snickered, and dove in.

The redhead had announced her pregnancy to the group of Guardians after her mate, Storm, had put Furio in a headlock for teasing her about eating more than usual one night at dinner.

True, she had quite the appetite, but she was a she-Wolf now, and Elena was sure that was pretty fucking ordinary. Still, males were always so dramatically protective of their mates' feelings.

Especially when their mates were expecting. Elena gasped at the sudden punch of pain she felt in her gut. Would she ever have a male of her own to worry over her that way? She didn't need anyone to defend her, but still. It might be nice.

Expecting a cub or pup was definitely cause for celebration. Elena unconsciously touched her own flat stomach, a gesture that did not go unnoticed by the other three women. She was frowning too. Hard.

Her heat cycle aside, Elena was not expecting a cub. And she would not be. Not for a very long while, if ever. The purpose of a feline Shifter's heat cycle was to ensure the survival of the species. Unlike other Shifters, felines did not always wait for their mates, fated or otherwise, before engaging in procreation.

And that was because of one simple fact. There were fewer feline Shifters than other subspecies, and therefore, evolution ensured procreation would not wait for increasingly rare matings to occur. Survival was key, and as always, nature found a way.

But Elena had always refused to be controlled by her evolutionary hormones. Her heat cycle was not now or ever going to control her life.

"Come on, El. We know something is up. You haven't been the same since you went out that night and came back many, *many* hours later," Holley said.

"Yeah, talk to us," Jessenia coaxed.

"And let us know if we have to cut someone's dick off. Cause we will," Fergie nodded, pointing her ice cream dripping spoon at her.

Elena snorted. She stood up, then sat down again, hard, on and empty chaise and stared at the three very different women. It was amazing they'd found each other, accepted one another, and formed this tremendous friendship. Even more amazing they insisted on including her regardless of how she protested and tried to resist.

"We are your girls, El. We got your back always. Don't you forget it." Fergie narrowed her eyes, and it was as if she was reading her thoughts and not for the first time, either.

"Spill," the redheaded she-Wolf insisted.

"You, uh, know I hooked up the other night, right?"

"Really? How was it?" Holley asked, eyes shining with glee.

"OMG! Holley, pregnancy has made you such a horn dog! Seriously though, did he make you come, right? Did he go down on you? Cause if he didn't, and that is the problem, we can straighten his ass out," Jessenia exclaimed.

"What? No!" Elena gasped.

"No, he did go down on you, or no, he didn't?" Fergie asked.

"Ladies! Please!" Elena yelled, and this time she was blushing. "Look, I met a guy, and everything was fine in the bed department, though we didn't really make it to the bed---"

"Woot Woot! So, what's his name?" Holley asked, swaying side to side on her feet, something she said eased the babe inside her belly.

"Oh. Um. I don't really know," Elena replied, ignoring the wide-eyed stares of the women.

"That's okay," Fergie said, nodding encouragingly. "She is a modern woman. This was a one night thing, right?"

"That's the thing though," Elena said, swallowing down her trepidation.

If she couldn't be honest with them, then their friendship was doomed. Might as well spill the beans.

"What is it, love?" Holley asked.

"My Panther kinda thinks he belongs to us, well, to *me*."

"Come again?" Holley asked.

"Damn straight she wants to come again," snorted Fergie.

"Shh. I think she's serious," Jessenia added.

"I am serious," Elena confessed. "I think the human I spent the night with might be my mate."

Mine.

Chapter Five

A pregnant hush settled over the *Ladies' Room*.

Holley's eyes filled with unshed tears, presumably happy ones since a wide grin spread across her face. Jessenia blinked her eyes, then looked at the other two females before looking back at Elena. As for Fergie, the redhead stood up and placed her half-filled carton of ice cream on the floor.

Uh oh. That was serious. Elena exhaled, relieved at her impromptu confession, and anxious at their reactions. Her Panther seemed quite pleased that she'd at least admitted to the possibility of the pretty human belonging to them.

Heaven knew he was pretty. Tall and rodeo

cowboy lean with wicked hazel eyes that burned with passion when he'd touched her, skilled lips, and talented hands. He was a work of fucking art. Literally.

Of course, Elena didn't know how to respond to the stunned silence that greeted her. The trio of females always had something to say, but now they looked as shocked as she felt.

Was it so unthinkable that she would have a male of her own? As it stood, she was not even sure about it. Not 100%. After all, it could all be some residual effect of all the fabulous fucking for all she knew, and she said as much.

"Elena, I am so happy for you," Holley grinned.

"Yeah. Congrats on the fab fucking," Fergie added.

"Fergie, you are so crude! Anyway, where'd you meet Mr. Wonderful?" Jess asked.

"Uh, I met him at that club with the good music by the train station. It's called *Midnight's*," Elena replied, relieved she knew the answer to that question.

"Does he work there?" the kitchen Witch continued her line of questioning, but Elena couldn't do more than shrug.

"I mean, not really. He was in the band---"

"OMG! You picked up a rocker? How cool! Was he tattooed? Did he have piercings? Did you use condoms? Those guys are usually whores,"

Fergie squealed, then slapped a hand over her mouth.

"Fergie!" Jessenia shook her head at her big-mouthed BFF.

"Um, sorry, about that last part," Fergie grimaced.

"Okayyyy. Well, no to the piercings. Yes, one tattoo. On his left side," she said, biting her lip as she recalled the beautiful ink that covered his body from right under his arm down his hip.

"What of?"

"Well," Elena blushed, remembering how she'd traced the ink with her hands, then lips.

Seemed like kismet now. So sleek and beautiful. Her one night stand man had a black panther tattooed down his side.

Of all the things in the world, she sighed, thinking about how warm and delicious his skin had tasted beneath her searching mouth. The second she'd spied the artwork, her inner kit had growled possessively at the sight. A truly magnificent piece, but more so, it had called to her beast.

"So, a panther, huh? And you somehow doubt

he's yours?" Jessenia made a face like Elena was crazy and shook her head.

"It's the way he responded to me that was kind of scary, I guess."

"Like how?"

"Did he hurt you?' Fergie stood up, a snarl in her throat.

"No! Of course not," chided Elena. "It was like he was really into me. He kept kissing me and touching me, and I mean we came together again and again, and he never seemed to get tired. And yes, before you ask *Moms*, he wore protection. The thing is that doesn't happen very often. Not to me."

"But you're a knockout, El," Fergie said. "How can guys not want to take you home and bang you all night long? I mean, if I was a guy, I'd be all over that!"

"Uh, thanks?" Elena said, but it came out more question. Jessenia was patting Fergie's arm and shaking her head.

"What? I mean it. Look at her for fuck's sake."

"I hate to admit this," Holley began. "But Fergie has a point. What kind of guys have you been dating, Elena?'"

"I haven't. Not lately, anyway. But I always choose supes to see me through my heat when the potions don't work. Typically, they are standoffish. I think I threaten them. And I never dated a normal."

"Never?"

"Nope. Never had time. I made my pledge to the Guardians when I was still a teenager."

"Wow. You were so young, El."

"No, it's cool. I love my job. But you know *why* I went out. Anyway, I don't know. My Panther might just be confusing my heat cycle with whatever hormones go off when you find your mate, right?" Elena asked, looking at the three stunned females.

As she tried talking it out, the more likely it seemed that the male she'd gone home with was just some guy who, while gifted in bed, *or against the wall and on the floor as it were*, was most likely not her fated mate. It was just good sex. Period.

"Only one way to tell for sure," Fergie said after a few long minutes had passed.

"What way?" Elena asked.

"Go see him."

"What? I can't do that!"

"Sure, you can. It's Thursday. He might be at the bar tonight, rocking out on his guitar."

"Bass."

"What?"

"He plays bass."

"I see," Fergie said, eyes twinkling. "Looks like you already know more about him than you think. You like him."

"I do not---"

"Do too. Suck it up, buttercup. Go see him."

"No, I---"

But the more she resisted, the more the ladies argued this was her only recourse. They were probably right. She needed to find out for herself if this was a fluke or not.

"First, you need to get changed," Fergie instructed, grabbing some things off the rack.

"No, I can just wear this," she said, gesturing towards her old jeans and tank top.

"She did not just say that. Please tell me she did not just say that," Fergie sighed dramatically.

"It's no use, El. Ever since *Little Miss Woof Woof* here has gotten herself knocked up, she's been crazier than ever," Jessenia mock whispered.

"*Shyaddap*," Fergie barked at her BFF, then turned to Elena.

"Sweetie, what you need is something that says fun, flirty, and up for fucking."

"I don't think---"

"Good! I never do," Fergie said, slapping Jessenia's hand when the woman agreed.

"Ooh, I know, I know. She needs something naughty!" Holley chimed in, and before she knew it, they'd started tossing items out at her and giving her orders to get dressed.

Scary bitches, for sure. But they were her scary bitches.

"Guys, I look like some fetishy freak in this outfit."

"Uh uh. You look totally *hawt*," Fergie said, and winked.

Dammit. Despite all her protests, Elena found herself in a short plaid skirt and a fuzzy maroon sweater that brought out the unusual hue of her eyes. Paired with knee high leather boots, she had to admit she felt a little like a cosplayer.

At the same time, Elena's confidence sure was boosted. At least the heels were flat, not like the ones she'd worn last time.

Elena jumped in her metallic black 1966 Jaguar XJ13. She loved the sports car, and though, it was for personal use, it had all the bells and whistles.

Her Jaguar had been modified with such perks as bulletproof glass, reinforced body, supped up tires and shocks to withstand ridiculously high speeds, and other goodies to counter attacks from their enemies.

With what was left of the Loyalists in hiding, things had been rather quiet for the Guardians of late. Elena quickly cleared her mind of any such thoughts, as there were some who believed in superstition.

Like firefighters and law enforcement officers, their supernatural counterparts, the Enforcers and Guardians of Chaos, rarely liked to mention quiet spells in their line of work.

Elena gunned the engine. She must have been nervous to be having such thoughts. Ridiculous. What did she have to worry about?

Confident that she had his interest, at least she did the other night, there was no reason for the human to ignore her. Surely this trip was not for no reason. And maybe, just maybe, he'd be up for another round or three?

Licking her lips, she pushed her sports car harder, making the trip in even less time than usual. Sure, her heat was over, but the truth was Elena's body tingled just thinking about the devastatingly handsome man.

With his dark hair so carelessly loose around his face, the man should have looked messy or just plain shaggy. But to her, he simply looked hot. He had the most gorgeous hazel green eyes flecked with gold, that if she didn't know better, Elena would have assumed made him part Big Cat Shifter. Tiger or maybe Leopard, but nope, he was all human.

His rodeo cowboy build meant long, powerful legs, a solid six pack for his abs, and nicely formed pecs. He had light swirls of dark hair on his chest, and she liked the feel of it against her skin. The man was the stuff her dreams were made of, and that was just his looks.

Never mind the fact he'd given her the best sex of her life. Hell, he'd made her see stars with that amazingly gifted body of his. But it was more than the sex that had her going back to *Midnight's*, that cold winter's evening.

Tingles of anticipation traveled up and down her spine at light speed. Maybe Fergie, Holley, and Jess were right about this. Maybe Elena should consider getting to know the human a little better. After all, if she was still thinking about him all this time later, he must be worth a second glance.

Mind made up, she squeezed her car into a tight little parking spot outside the bar, almost blocking the alley. Nerves threatened to assail her, but she took a fortifying breath, checked her face and hair, then got out of the car. And that was when she got a whiff of the unthinkable.

Blood. *His.*

"You're coming with us!"

Thwack! Crash!

"Fuck you-oof!"

"Should have come quietly," a dark, sinister voice snarled.

"I said, fuck you."

Her supernaturally enhanced hearing picked up on some of the heated exchange. The blows were hard enough to draw blood, and her she-Cat was beyond pissed having recognized the spicy tang of her male's life force.

The last sentence uttered was deep and raspy, the responding remark riddled with pain and famil-iar. Elena sniffed, trying to get a lead on what she was about to face.

Gila Shifters. Grrr. And from the sound of it, they had her man.

Mine.

Her Panther snarled loudly in her mind's eye, the beast ready to obliterate anyone or thing that harmed a hair on her mate's head. Mate? Fuck. She didn't have time to debate the rightness of the state-ment with her inner feline. He needed her.

That was her last thought before she took off running into the dark alley. She sent a text to the rest of the Guardians, before shoving her cell phone back in the pocket of her ridiculous skirt. Not waiting for a reply, she shoved off the short bomber jacket she wore and readied herself to face the enemy. Elena wasn't going to wait for back up. Not when he could be hurt.

"Stop resisting," Lizard breath hissed into her human's ear, but the man put up a fight.

"Look guys, I'm flattered by your interest, but I am involved with someone else."

Lip bloodied, her human grinned and shoved one foul Gila Shifter off of him. The Shifter recoiled angrily, while his body brought his hand back, ready to swing.

"Hey there, asshole," Elena said, having snuck up behind him, she held his wrist and spun him around to face her.

"I guess you're going first," she growled, then struck him hard in the solar plexus with her fist, followed by a roundhouse kick to his jaw.

"You!" Her human gasped, then turned to jump in front of her when another one of the Lizard men tossed a brick her way.

"No!" Elena yelled, as she watched him take the hit meant for her.

Anger coursed through her, and she snarled at

the soon to be dead fuckers who'd touched her guy. Poor, beautiful, brave normal. She grabbed the Lizard who threw the brick and lifted him over her head, tossing him into two others who'd come out of the shadows.

While they scrambled to regroup, she lifted her normal up and lowered him behind some garbage cans to keep him out of harm's way. She heard them the second they identified her and turned to face the Loyalist scum.

"She's a Guardian! Get her!"

Offner was gone, but his supporters remained and the war to protect magic was always raging. Was Elena selfish for laying this all at his feet? She wondered, thinking of the human bleeding for her on the floor.

Shit. She couldn't do this now. The Gila Shifters were getting their venom ready, she could see it in the way their glands swelled, readying to release the poisonous secretions. Fight first, think later.

Roar!

Chapter Six

ours earlier...

It had been a shitty week all around for Logan. After waking up delightfully exhausted and hopeful for maybe another bout of hot as fuck sex, he'd discovered the pink eyed vixen had run out on him.

As if that wasn't bad enough, he'd spent the whole weekend trying to run down the victim of the warehouse bombing's next of kin to see if he couldn't ask for a blood sample to rule out his impossible findings. But John Doe had not been claimed by anyone, so that was out.

Starting from scratch, Logan had put a few more samples from regular run of the mill blood donors through his tests to rule out whether something in his equipment was tainted. Those passed with flying colors, so it had to have been the sample. But for some reason, it bothered him.

Everything about the blood appeared normal. Except for one thing. A burn victim with that level of injury should have shown signs of acute blood loss and anemia. But that blood was not only normal. It was better than normal. Under his watchful eye he watched John Doe's blood cells regenerate like something out of a sci-fi flick.

Logan should have destroyed the samples, but he didn't. He'd held on to them even after Margo replied to his monthly email check in, with her standard *get rid of that bullshit and reevaluate your life* message.

She had little time for his insistence that sometimes things were simply inexplicable. Margo preferred cold hard facts. Still, he enjoyed hearing from his twin. It was like a balm for his wounded ego, though he wasn't even sure why he mentioned his one night stand.

Why are you wasting time on this woman? She's obviously some nympho groupie. Did you use a condom? I hope you did, brother of mine, otherwise I'd watch out for a letter from some lawyer demanding child support. Stay safe and always wear a hat on your little head!

Fucking Margo. Blunt as hell, but he loved her. As if that bit of humiliation wasn't enough, he was worried about showing up at *Midnight's* on Thursday. He'd pissed off Elliot by walking out on them last week, but the band's front man had swallowed his pride while the other members simply shrugged and high-fived Logan on his score.

She'd been hot alright. Unbelievably sexy and seductive as hell, but sweet and vulnerable, too. In a way that made his cock throb in need, and his heart thud with emotion. He tried to just smile and accept the joshing over the mega hot babe who'd rocked his world then left him high and dry. Well, he was not crying in his cereal exactly, but close enough.

Fuck.

He didn't even know her name. But there had been something about her from the very beginning that drew him to her like a moth to a flame. What the hell was all that about anyway? Logan Wells did not do starry-eyed lover very well.

He had women, sure. But his work was the thing. His research was the reason behind everything he did. Sometimes he went weeks without coming up for air, except for Thursday nights. That was when he always reserved a few hours to unwind and let his thoughts just flow through the notes he banged out on his bass.

But this female had him tied up in knots, for fuck's sake. He was seriously borderline pathetic.

The woman hadn't even bothered to give him her name. hell, she hadn't spoken more than five words to him, and those were mainly *yes* and *harder*. Not that he'd minded.

Still, a guy felt a little used after a week flew by and no call, no note, no nothing. Shit. He was a total pussy.

Growling to himself, he took an Uber to the club, his *Rickenbacker* in its case. Teaching himself to play bass had been the smartest thing Logan had done with his time between AP classes back in high school.

A person with his kind of scientifically geared brain needed creative outlets otherwise he'd implode. Found that out the hard way when one of his best professors from school had told him of his attempted suicide over the pressure of being enrolled in some of Princeton's most advanced classes and getting his first pubic hair.

High pressure indeed. Logan had listened when his professor advised him not to get lost in the science, to remember that he was human. Music did that for him. It allowed him to connect with other people when that was something that had been difficult for him his whole life.

Music had given him a reason to be seen by the cool kids. Made him appealing to women. Hell, it still got him laid. Frowning as he got out of the Uber, Logan pushed all thoughts of pink eyed seductresses from his mind. He was ready to play himself into oblivion.

Fess up, brother, you're looking for her.

No, he was not waiting for her to arrive. No, he did not scan the crowd repeatedly for a flash of pink eyes or long ivory legs in a sinfully short mini skirt.

Liar liar.

When the band halted for their break, Elliot had started to give him some shit about disappearing, but Logan was in no mood. He grabbed his tumbler of iced tea and headed to the alley for some cold but fresh air.

The atmosphere in the bar had gone stale, and he was counting the minutes till he could get his sorry ass home. What he needed was a few weeks uninterrupted in his lab. Then he could forget about pink eyed blondes who tasted like bubble gum and made him come so hard his eyes crossed.

He leaned against the brick wall, grateful it was winter, and he couldn't smell whatever usual suspects were undoubtedly fouling up the alley. Newark was known for being a grungy, rough and tumble city, but it was doing its best to clean shit up. Like downtown Jersey City, Weehawken, and Hoboken had years earlier.

Still, perhaps he'd been foolish to wander outside despite Rick going on break. The burly bouncer was a good guy, quiet for the most part.

"So, Dr. Wells, about your research, I had some questions for you." Harry, one of the regulars at *Midnight*, stepped out of the shadows, startling Logan into almost dropping his glass.

"Geez, Harry, you almost gave me a heart attack," Logan replied, shaking his head.

This guy could not take a hint. When he'd first approached Logan and said he'd recognized him from work, he'd smiled and nodded. Hell, he'd responded politely to his inquiries about where Logan had gone after leaving big pharma, and what he'd been up to.

Typically, Logan did not discuss his current research projects with anyone. Especially, since he hadn't exactly acquired his samples on the up and up. Knowing a few first responders who needed extra cash was helpful in that respect. He was able to acquire samples after the fact, and never ever at someone's expense. His research was groundbreaking, or it could be, as long as he didn't violate his NDA.

"Sorry, Harry, I am not talking shop tonight," Logan replied and shook his head.

"I'm afraid Dr. Wells, you do not have a choice."

The man smiled, and for the first time Logan noticed something very strange about his eyes. The slime green color was off putting, but the vertical pupil and corresponding eyelids were downright weird.

A few more men with similar coloring and equally disturbing eyes came out of the shadows, bracketing Harry on either side. Logan began to think this was a really bad fucking idea.

"What do you want?" He placed the glass on the ground and braced himself for the impending skirmish.

Logan was not big on physical scuffles, but he knew when one was about to happen. He changed his stance, bringing his left shoulder up to block his face and his right side back.

Not the best athlete, he was always a damn good student. One of the first boxing lessons his grandfather had given him was on the correct way to stand. Elbows against his chest, chin down, ready to defend. It seemed wrong at first, but Grandfather had insisted.

"Elbows down against your chest. Protect your face. Never drop your hands. Put your body behind your punch."

The old bastard was good at two things, making money and boxing. And he'd taught Logan well. With his Orthodox stance perfected, he had maximum torque and leverage. He could hit harder and react faster. Logan had been taught well how to defend himself.

But still, he was worried. Outnumbered and in the dark, freezing alley, it was a long shot. Still, he wasn't going down without a fight.

"You're coming with us!"

One of the men said pointing a long, spindly finger at Logan. There was something off about these guys. They were all really tall, and from a six and a half foot man, that was saying something. Tall and fast too. They way they moved unnaturally quick, and, what the fuck? One of them was clinging to the far brick wall like a fucking spider!

"Come along. Don't fight us, *Wellssss*," Harry hissed.

Oh yeah. Something was totally fucked about the guy. Logan noticed his skin taking on a greenish hue. That was quickly followed by a foul odor permeating the cold air.

"No, go ahead. Fight *ussss*," another said, and before Logan could refuse, the second stepped forward and punched him in the gut, then the bastard spit right in his face.

Thwack! Spit! Punch! Kick!

Pain exploded throughout Logan's entire body. He doubled forward then back with each blow. The place where the fucker had hocked a loogie on him started to burn, and he did his best to wipe it off, spitting blood onto the ground.

Anger burned in his veins, and something else too. Was it guilt? No, regret, loss, sadness over not seeing the bubble gum eyed beauty once more. If only he could've met her again.

Dammit. Why the hell was he thinking about her at a time like this? Logan was getting his ass handed to him, and he was starting to feel very dizzy.

"Ready to come along quietly, now?" Harry asked.

"Fuuuck youuu-oof!" His speech was slurred, that wasn't good. Add in another blow to his chin, and he was looking at a probable concussion.

Logan's head snapped back. He was an okay boxer, but these guys were something else. No matter how many times he struck, they kept on coming. Like his blows were nothing to them.

It was a little emasculating, but he chalked it up to steroids or PCP, some drug or something. Fuck, when did they all start turning green?

There was no way he could take on those two by himself. The truth hurt sometimes. Even more than a punch to the stomach.

"Should have come quietly," one of the men he didn't know said in a dark, sinister voice.

"I said, fuck you." Logan sneered, spitting directly in the man's face, then using his booted foot to slam down hard on the man's instep, then he drove his fist into his stomach, and watched in horror as the man smiled revealing three inch long fangs oozing slime.

"What the fuck are you?" Logan gasped, but before anyone could answer, something sleek and fast ran into them.

"Hey there, asshole," a familiar voice said to the man attempting to hit him yet again.

Shit. She was there! His mystery beauty of the bubble gum eyes. But this was dangerous. No! He needed her gone.

"Stay back!" Logan yelled out towards where he thought the mystery woman was standing, earning him another punch from the man-thing nearest him.

His vision was hazy and for some reason he felt numb on the left side of his body, but he felt it when her pink gaze landed on him. He didn't know why she was there, but she was not happy.

That was obvious in the way she took in his condition from head to toe. He must have been pretty fucked up because whatever she saw, it clearly angered her. The woman turned, a snarl on her pretty mouth as she spun to face his two assailants.

Words were exchanged, and he was having a hell of a hard time following. Fear for her safety outweighed the pain he felt, and he tried once again to tell her to go. Shit. His voice was not obeying him.

From the corner of his eye, he saw one of Harry's green goons reach on the ground for something. Was it a brick? Horrified at the thought of anyone marring her beautiful skin, Logan tried his best to warn her.

"This isn't your concern," hissed one of the men.

"Really? And that's your call, tough guy?"

Before Logan could say anything, she moved into a crouching attack position like something from one of those old Kung Fu movies he enjoyed. Then she started to kick some serious ass, but not before the sneaky fucker with the brick inched closer. Finally, Logan launched himself in front of her with one final burst of adrenaline.

The brick made impact with the back of his skull and Logan had never felt such intense pain. The woman caught him as he stumbled, lowered him behind some garbage cans.

"Stay here," she whispered, touching the side of his face.

Shit. He couldn't just lie there, though. He had to do something, but he was losing feeling in his body. Terrified and unable to move like he wanted, Logan tried to trace what had happened. None of the injuries he'd received could've made him paralyzed. No. It had to have been something in that goon's spit.

Fascinating. And also, pretty fucking impossible.

"She's a Guardian, you idiots!" Harry yelled, attempting to grab Logan from behind the trash cans.

He started to drag him down the alley, surprisingly strong for a short, stunted looking man, but Logan was not going anywhere without a fight. Mustering all his strength, he turned and grabbed for something, anything on the alley floor.

Finding his iced tea glass, he closed his bruised and somewhat numb fingers over the cold hard container and smashed it right over that fucker Harry's head. He listened for the man's stunned scream to make sure he'd hit him, then Logan scrambled away from the jackoff.

He needed to find his mystery woman and get her the hell out of there. What was she doing? Coming to his fucking rescue it seemed, and wasn't that emasculating?

Shit. He didn't give a fuck about that, and if he could have, he would have laughed. Right then though, he was pretty sure his vocal cords were slowly freezing, like he was paralyzed by something. Whatever odd chemical was in that spit, he concluded.

Logan was all for equal rights between the sexes, but he did not want her tangled up in whatever psychotic plan Harry had for kidnapping him. What was the weird man up to and who was behind the attack?

Probably some big pharmaceutical company or government agency. They were always after Logan for his research, but he'd walked away from that a long time ago. His left leg began to twitch and slow, and he cursed roughly.

As a biochemist he hoped some of that fucking spit was still on his clothes for later research, but again that was something he wasn't all too concerned with at the moment. He scanned for the woman with his one still working eye and watched in awe as she lifted up one of the attackers and tossed him into a brick wall.

Holy fucking shit.

The female was a total badass. If he wasn't worried sick over her getting injured because of him, he would so have a hard on right then. Not that he needed to worry. Apparently, she was a better fighter than those green fucking bozos.

And she looked hot doing it. Fuck. He really needed to rein in his crazy lust-filled thoughts where the stranger was concerned. He crawled to where the woman was beating the shit out of one of the other men.

Blood poured from a wound on her stomach and Logan saw red. He grabbed the foot of the tall stool Rick, *Midnight's* bouncer, usually sat on, and used all his remaining strength to lift it and bash it over another assailant's head. He might be down, but he refused to just watch while she fought for him.

More men came running down the alley. One with long hair streaming behind him while smoke appeared out of his nostrils. There was another dark-haired man, and he held some sort of glowing blue flashlight that exploded as he punched one of the attackers dead in the jaw.

Just when Logan thought he was about to pass out, he rolled onto his back. And that's when he knew the spit not only had a paralytic but some kind of hallucinogenic as well. With a mighty roar that seemed to shake the very alley, Logan's one good eye widened as he tried to make out the shape coming straight towards him from the sky.

No fucking way.

It was a Dragon. Not some lizard they threw the tag on to make it sound cooler. A real fucking Dragon. A huge mythological *knight in shining armor eating* Dragon. And it was circling the sky above the alley behind *Midnight's*.

Some more green hued men joined the fray, and Logan wondered how these men all had the same genetic makeup that would grant that strange color scheme. He started to lose focus as more and more of his body went numb. Maybe this was all some kind of crazy trip, he wondered as another flash of fire came blasting out of the Dragon's maw.

"Stay down!"

The pink eyed beauty ordered, and he tried. Really, he did. But some fucker was creeping in on her and he had no choice but to try and protect her.

Swinging out with what remained of the stool, he caught the asshole in the back of the knees. The mystery woman growled, her head snapping back and gaze catching his. She grabbed the attacker as he tripped and slammed his head on the asphalt. He was down for now, but Logan had a feeling it wouldn't be for long.

"I said down," she snapped at Logan, crouching low in front of him in a defensive position.

Dizzy and out of sorts, Logan took a moment to appreciate her long, powerful build as she kicked some serious ass. Snarls and growls came from the remaining attackers. He was feeling weak and dizzy, and at this point, doubted he could lift any part of himself off the ground.

He'd wanted to see her again so badly. But like this? Shit. Not what he'd planned.

"Hey, are you okay?"

Her husky voice sounded so sweet and concerned as her bubble gum gaze found his eyes. Damn, was she beautiful. He wished he could speak or reach out for her, but Logan was too far gone.

Eyes closing, he went down for the count. But he could've sworn she held him and whispered to him, as she lifted him out of the alley.

"*I got you.*"

Chapter Seven

" In my office now," growled Kingston.

The big Diamond Dragon, and Alpha of their group of Guardians, was used to being listened to. So, when Elena showed signs of hesitating, he turned to snarl angrily at her from the corridor of the Keep. Even had white smoke puffing out of his nostrils.

"My love, is there a reason you are going all Dragony in the hallway?"

"Holley," Kingston said, turning towards his fated mate with all the love he felt evident on his face.

"Nothing that concerns you, *conpar*. It's just Guardian business."

"I see," she replied, moving past him to enter the

infirmary where Elena was standing over the unconscious male she'd brought back with her.

"Elena, may I?" Holley smiled and gestured for
her to move aside, but her inner kitty really was not
cool with that idea.

"I promise not to hurt him, I merely want to
check his wounds."

"Uh, yeah sure," she mumbled in response, but
her she-Cat was growling softly, and there was
nothing she could do to mask the sound.

Fuck.

The feline was possessive already, and all her
suspicions about the human male and what he was to
her started filling her head. Still, she felt like an idiot.

Holley was fully mated, pregnant, and in no way
a threat. She grabbed her inner kitty by the ruff and
pushed the beast back down. The normal looked
pale and his vitals were not great. Worry and anxiety
filled her till she thought she would choke on it.

Elena had never been so afraid, and that was
positively galling. She'd always been a loner, a
badass, a tough as fuck female. But here she was,
practically in tears over one puny human!

Dammit. That wasn't fair. He'd been brave and
protective. He'd come after her to try and fight the
Gila Shifters, though he did not know what he was

up against. He wanted to save her, even though she more than likely got him into this mess. And that was the real problem. Elena felt guilty.

Jessenia filed in soon after, along with Byram, the only Vampire in their group and the one with the most knowledge when it came to healing injuries.

"Elena, he will be okay. Go now with Kingston and the others, I will let you know if we need you," Holley spoke directly to her, voicing all of Elena's unspoken concerns while ignoring her own grumbling mate.

If anyone could handle the Dragon, it was the otherworldly Witch. To think Holley had been imprisoned behind the walls of the Keep for hundreds of years before Kingston had rescued her, boggled the she-Cat's mind. Holley was one of them now. A Guardian's *conpar* or most sacred fated mate. Elena not only respected her, but she loved the Witch too.

She looked into Holley's eyes and Elena gave in. The Witch would keep him safe. Even her Panther acknowledged he was in better hands with the two Witches and the Vampire, though she hissed a warning to all three as she left the room reluctantly.

Kingston stalked behind his desk and waited until all were present. Furio, Storm, the Dragon himself, Elena, and finally, Egros stood in the Alpha's office. Her face remained impassive while Kingston rattled off the standard questions.

"Furio and Storm were tracking the Loyalists when we got your text," Kingston said in his Alpha voice. "What I want to know, is what were you doing there? You were not out on a mission tonight."

"No, I was not. I was there on personal business," she replied, noting with unease the four pairs of male eyes on her.

"So, you didn't know the Gilas would be there?"

"No, sir."

"Well, why the hell didn't you wait for backup?"

"They were attacking, sir."

"A normal? You risked exposure for a normal."

"Sir, I could not let them take him. They were trying to kidnap him maybe to use him as leverage to get to---"

"To get to who?"

"Me!" She yelled, startling herself and those in the room. No one had ever raised their voice to Kingston Baldric. Except now.

"Why?" The Dragon asked in a deceptively level tone.

"He and I...*we*, that is," she stuttered. "It is personal, sir.:

"Elena, you ignored our most basic instruction to keep normals out of this war. You engaged in a supernatural battle with the human present. Then you brought him here when an emergency room would have sufficed. Why, Elena?" Kingston asked, his stance unbending.

"No, sir, he was hit with Gila venom. He needs our help. And the truth is, I was there to meet---"

"Who could be so important you risked outing our secrets?" Kingston glared at her as he spoke, his anger palpable.

"I'll tell you what she was doing," Egros interrupted, the Witch's eyes flashing angrily at her.

She stepped back, shocked by the emotion she saw there. Elena tried to gather her thoughts, but Egros was already moving forward. The male Witch was vibrating with anger, and while her heat was not exactly a secret, she could not believe he was about to share her personal matters with all of them.

"Eg, no---"

"She was in heat. The potions Holley and I have been making to manage it, are not cutting it anymore. Elena went to work through her heat cycle with some human," he spat the word as if it disgusted him, and that hurt worse than any blow.

"Egros, you have no right," she said, fighting the rage that threatened to spill over and consume her.

Egros was a Guardian, like her. Her friend, or so she had thought. How could he do this? Humiliation warred with fury, but she kept a tight rein on both.

"*I* have no right? You had no right. A human, El? A weak human over---"

"Over you? Is that what you were going to say? You were never in the running, Eg! Never!" She shouted the words cruelly, wishing she could take them back as soon as they'd slipped from her mouth.

The tension in the richly furnished room was thick and irritating. The Keep seemed to sense it, and the lights brightened for a moment, causing them all to step back and blink.

"That's enough!" Kingston roared.

"Yes, it is enough. I did what I had to do, Kingston. Punish me or not, it is your call, Alpha." She spoke directly to the Dragon, ignoring the other males in the room.

He blinked and paced, shrugging in his discomfort. She knew what he needed to ask and waited.

"So, you went through, uh, your heat with the human?"

"Yes, sir," she stated and turned to the Witch who was standing, eyes widened in shock as if he realized what he did. Maybe he had. Either way, it was too late.

"I made the mistake of thinking Egros was my friend and confided in him about my cycle---"

"Elena, I am your friend, but you risked a lot for this *normal*---"

"No. You risked our friendship by spilling details of my personal life in this conference room that is reserved for Guardian business. You had no right to tell anyone anything concerning me and my choices," she replied with quiet dignity.

Her heart was pounding, her inner feline scratching at her skin. The Panther wanted out. She was angry at Egros, annoyed with Kingston, ambivalent about the other two, but more than anything, she wanted to be in the infirmary.

With him.

"Elena, I am sorry about this. It is grossly unfair that a female should have her personal life under a microscope---"

"It should not matter that I am female, Kingston. None of the males here are subject to scrutiny when they fall into bed with someone," she replied through gritted teeth.

"I agree that Egros overstepped, but what you do

as a Guardian has consequences," Kingston began, but she cut him off.

"Yes, he did. I am no different than any of you," she said, meeting each male's gaze in the closed space.

Never before had she felt such anger at her fellow Guardians, but this was bullshit. Shifters were notorious for guarding their females, but sometimes it could be a little claustrophobic. Not to mention hypocritical.

"Furio, Storm, and even you, Kingston, are guilty of going even farther than I have with this man. What I did for him, any of you would have done for your females!"

"Elena," Storm said, attempting to intercede.

"I'm not finished yet," Elena snapped, growling at the Wolf.

"None of you have any right to my private life or my personal matters. Even if I hadn't slept with him, this male is the victim of a Gila Shifter attack---"

"That he wouldn't have been involved in if not for you," Kingston replied.

"No. You are wrong. What I was doing there doesn't change the facts, Kingston. They were after him, not me."

"What?"

Chapter Eight

The Diamond Dragon's mouth fell open as he began to connect the dots Elena had been so desperately trying to arrange for him. Egros was a jealous fool, and she could forgive him that. But not if the Witch put her human in danger because of his own stupidity.

"You heard me," Elena said with slightly better control of her emotions.

"I didn't put him in danger. I *found* him in danger. Furthermore, I acted as any of you would have done, in the *victim's* best interest," she said, her voice getting stonier by the second.

"You brought a human here," Egros seethed, but a growl from Storm had the Witch zipping his lips tightly.

Though Fergie had changed to Wolf after he'd bitten her, Storm was still a little touchy about the whole human Shifter prejudice thing that, unfortunately, was very real. The Guardians protected magic for all, but Elena supposed she'd never really thought about how some of them felt about humans. Clearly, it was something they needed to discuss.

"Look, Kingston," she said, choosing to speak to her Alpha and not the group at large. "The man needed help, I brought him here. Anything that happened between us previously is none of your business."

"Elena, your heat cycle is personal, I agree, but--_"

"No buts, Kingston. A Shifter's heat is painful, hell, it is downright unbearable if not sated. That is simple biology. But it doesn't make me less of a Guardian."

"Of course not, I only meant there are protocols--_"

"Bullshit. Males go into something very similar to rut and it has never been acknowledged as a negative. Besides, none of you need time off when that happens. You simply fuck at will."

The men in the room winced and looked anywhere but at Elena. She had a point, and they knew it. It was chauvinistic at best to celebrate a male Guardian's prowess when his hormones demand he sate his lust between the sheets, and to want to force a female to take a leave of absence for the same damn thing. Fuck that.

"You chose a human---" Egros spat, barely able to control himself.

"Easy, man," Furio said to the furious Witch.

"Elena, I am not judging you, and I don't think any of us should," Storm added, eyes narrowing at Egros.

"We just want you safe is all," Furio, the only Stallion Shifter among them, added.

"Thank you for that," she said, and shook her head. "But I am a warrior, *a Guardian of Chaos*, just like you. The fact is, I don't have to explain myself to any of you."

"The hell you don't---"

"Egros enough! Everyone, out. Now!" Kingston commanded. "Except you, Elena."

The three males left the room, leaving with their concern, anger, and sorrow. Thank goodness. Their emotions had been batting up against her through their Guardians' bonds, and she wasn't sure how much more she could take.

Aside from her father, who'd all but disowned

her when she left his house, Elena never had much family. It was oddly humbling to feel so much emotion from their group. But at the same time, she resented their interference.

"Elena, I hope you understand, we are all just worried about you."

"Worried? Why? Because I fucked someone, Kingston?"

"No! I mean, yes. I mean, shit," he shook his head and sighed heavily. "It's just---"

"When have any of the men in this group asked me who they can fuck, Kingston? You included. I am not a virgin. And I wasn't one when I met him."

Kingston watched her intently. He was a great leader, and occasionally knew when to be quiet, and when to interfere. Like now. He simply waited for her to speak, and she figured she owed him that much.

"Look, I went back to see him, and he was already under attack. That is the truth."

"I never doubted you, Elena. But why did you go back?" His voice calm and even, she saw no reason to deny his question.

"Because I needed to wait till after my heat was fully over to see if my Cat was right. To see if---" She paused, stumbling over the words, too emotional to give voice to what she was thinking.

Kingston gestured to his large leather couch, and she took direction, sitting down heavily. He poured them each three fingers of some old hard to read label of Scotch. After a few minutes, she sipped and allowed the smokey strong liquor to slide down her throat.

Shifters needed a lot of alcohol to get drunk. Even then, their metabolism burned through it rather quickly. It was the same conundrum that made the potions she was using to stave off her heat cycle becoming less and less effective.

"So," Kingston began, jogging her from her thoughts. "Come on, El, tell me why you really went back to that bar."

"I went back to see if my Panther was right," she replied, unable to lie to her Alpha. "To see, if he really is mine."

Kingston's shocked eyes met hers, and she couldn't be sure if that was happiness or shock on his face. The look swept across his features so briefly. Someone knocked on the office door, followed by a woman's voice.

"He's awake," Holley called before opening the door.

Elena sped past the pregnant Witch carefully and raced to the infirmary. The antiseptic smell was not unpleasant, and even better, was finding the same hauntingly familiar hazel eyes peeking up at her.

"Hi." Elena breathed the word, watching him for signs of pain or recognition.

He blinked slowly, pushing himself up, but wincing with pain as his hand reached up to touch the bandages on his head where he'd been whipped by one Gila Shifter's spiked tail. Holley had removed the poison and patched up the cuts, but he was human, after all, and healing would need time.

"Do you need help sitting up? A pillow? Water?"

"Your name."

"What?"

"I just need to know your name," the handsome stranger said as he lay back on his pillow.

His hair was tousled carelessly across his forehead, and his voice was hoarse and scratchy. But Elena never saw a better looking male in her entire life.

His shirt had been removed, and Elena's eyes flashed to the tattoo she knew was there but could barely see at present. The ink covering his side was big enough to wrap around the small of is back and some of his chest and abdomen too.

Elena's mouth watered just thinking about it. Entirely inappropriate considering how banged up he was. Still, she allowed her gaze to roam over him. So handsome. Lean and tall, muscular, but not overly so. His skin was fair, and his chest had a light smattering of dark hair.

"Elena," she said, licking her suddenly dry lips. "My name is Elena Soussa."

"Well, hello Elena," he said with a sexy smile on his face despite the bruises and his obvious exhaustion from whatever foul poison those fuckers had infected him with.

"Nice to finally know your name. I'm Logan. Logan Wells."

"Nice to meet you too," she said, grinning back. The man's smile was infectious.

"Wish you wouldn't go away, but I have to," he whispered, closing his eyes, and drifting back into oblivion.

Panic gripped her for a split second. Her heart constricted. How could she feel so strongly about a man she hardly knew? But she knew how. Even if she was not quite ready to say it aloud.

Elena turned her head to find Holley waiting

there with Kingston. She gestured for the woman to speak up, unable to do so as worry and unease coursed through her.

"Oh. He's fine, El. He will require lots of sleep, of course, but he will completely recover. I am almost positive."

"Oh, thank the gods. And thank you," Elena said, exhaling and nodding.

"Did he say anything?" Kingston asked.

"His name is Logan Wells," she returned.

"Okay, good," Kingston replied. "At least we have a place to start."

Chapter Nine

Logan tossed and turned. He was having the most messed up dream. Dragons and lizard men with spiked tails were fighting each other in a back alley in Newark.

Harry, the pesky bar fly, had tried to kidnap him. His beautiful bubble gum flavored stranger, the one who'd sexed him up and left his townhouse before he'd woken up after their night together, was there too.

Except instead of being the goddess of all things smexy, she was a badass superhero who'd saved his life. Fuck, she was so hot. But he knew that already. Logan's only regret was not knowing her name.

Elena. Elena Soussa.

The words suddenly appeared in his head, and

he frowned. How did he know that? Once more he heard them, whispered in his brain by her voice. More memory than made up.

Shit. When did she tell him her name? Why was he remembering it if she didn't? That's not how memories worked. His brain felt foggy, and his body burned with aches and pains never before felt. Something was wrong. Logan blinked.

The sudden influx of light hurt, and he groaned softly, aware of footsteps rushing towards him. Okay, so he was alive. And he was somewhere. What he didn't know was where. Fuck.

His head ached like mad. His body too. It was like he had the flu, but so much worse. Someone grabbed his head a little roughly, peeling his eyelids back they shined a penlight in one than the other.

"Ouch, fuck. Easy," he grumbled, but the strange man just grunted, and wrote something down.

"Are you a doctor? What hospital is this?" Logan asked, sitting up with no small amount of difficulty.

Shit.

He'd never felt so bad in all his life. The stranger didn't bother answering him, and that was when Logan began to get nervous. He looked around the room. Clean and sterile, but the mix of ancient medical technology with cutting edge was mysterious to say the least.

His clothes had been removed, and from the funk in his mouth, he guessed he'd been unconscious more than a night. As a scientist, he was not prone to hysteria, and yet, something in him was screaming that this was not right.

Logan squinted against the bright light shining over his head, and almost immediately it dimmed. Like the room was reading his thoughts.

Wow. Maybe he should think of the woman again.

"Um, excuse me," he tried to get the stranger's attention, but the man in black ignored him.

"Hello? I said excuse me," Logan managed a small smile when the uninterested stranger turned to acknowledge him.

"Thanks, uh, can you tell me the name of the hospital? Call my doctor? Or just, you know, talk to me?"

"Are you in pain?"

"What? No. Well, yes."

"I see. Is it excruciating?'

"No. Obviously," he replied dryly. "I feel like I am recovering from a bad case of the flu."

"Aches?"

"Yes."

"Mm hmm. Your name is Logan Wells? I see you are a geneticist and biochemist? But you were fired from---"

"I was not fired.! I left, but I signed an NDA, a non-disclosure agreement, so I can't give you any information without violating that."

"I see---"

"Oh, hello. You're awake!" A redheaded woman with a wide grin and dancing eyes wandered into the room. "Elena will be so happy. Hey Eg, what's up?"

She asked the angry little man who'd been pretty much an ass up till then.

"You got him?" The man called Eg asked, and the redhead nodded.

The female walked in and sat down in a lounge chair, kicking her shoes off. Well, he thought they were shoes, but to Logan, they looked like torture devices. The woman sighed loudly. She dropped a purse on the floor next to her shoes and rolled her ankles as if she'd been walking miles and miles.

Who knew? Maybe she had. Still, Logan was more interested in getting some answers. The redhead was cute, pleasant even, but she had nothing on a certain tall blonde who'd been haunting his dreams nonstop since he'd met her.

Was the woman, *Elena*, involved in some sort of fight protecting him, or had he imagined all that? He wished he had the answers. Not knowing was beginning to grate on his nerves.

Logan had never been overly emotional, but he felt panic blooming inside him as he thought of the worst possible scenarios.

Eaten by Dragon? Dragged away by Lizard men and made some kind of slave? Harry kidnapping her? Eeek! He needed answers!

Shit.

Was she okay? He needed to know, dammit. His heart raced at the thought of Elena hurt or in trouble.

And how the fuck do I know her name?

Images of her standing over him, concern in her pink gaze flashed through his mind, and he calmed a bit. Suddenly, he knew. Elena was okay. She'd been to see him, had told him her name.

Elena. Her name meant shining light. One of those useless bits of info his scientific mind stored away for whatever reason.

Logan repeated it in his mind, thinking he'd never heard anything so fitting, so perfect to describe her. From the silver platinum hair on her head to her alabaster skin and those hypnotic pink eyes. She was bright, beautiful, dynamite in bed, and from what he'd seen of her fighting skills, she was deadly as well.

He'd never met anyone like her and judging from the way she'd occupied most of his thoughts since he'd spent the night with her, he never would. The truth came blasting into his brain like it had been launched there by a rocket.

Shit.

The evidence supported his theory, and for once in his life, he could find nothing to contradict his findings. Crazy? Maybe. Odds that she reciprocated his feelings? Not good. Whatever. It wouldn't change the facts.

Logan was in love.

Somehow, some way, he'd fallen in love with a bubble gum pink eyed hottie who fought like Bruce Lee and fucked like a goddess.

Gulp.

His body reacted predictably to just the thought of her, and he adjusted his sheet and dropped a pillow on his lap, lest his visitor get the wrong idea.

There was no doubt about it. He was meant to be with Elena. But where was she now?

"Oh yeah, that's better," the redhead said, interrupting his shocking musings. She sighed contentedly now that her feet were free of her spiked heels.

"Why do you wear those things if they hurt?"

"What? Those aren't *things*, those are Louboutins!"

"What's a *Loo boo tin?*"

"OMG! Just *shhh*, okay? We're gonna take it down a notch cause getting upset is not good for the baby," she said more to herself than him.

Logan raised his eyebrows but decided to back off. He didn't grow up with his sister in the same household, but Margo was one fierce female when it came to anything she was passionate about.

Apparently, the redhead liked shoes. And Logan was smart enough to recognize something feral in the pregnant female. Especially when it came to her *Loo Boo Tins.*

Yikes.

Logan was all about self-preservation. Clearly, the woman was not to be fucked with when it came to her shoes. So, hands raised in surrender, he changed the subject.

"Uh, okay. My bad. Look, can you tell me where I am?"

"Oh, no worries. You're with us," she smiled, and he was pretty sure her incisors were a tad longer than a moment ago.

Gulp.

"Uh, so, who is us? And where is Elena?" Logan tried again with a non-threatening smile on his face.

He was getting antsier by the minute. Instant connection to his unbelievably hot, mystery woman aside, Logan had no fucking idea where he was or if he was safe. Though, he sincerely doubted she'd leave him somewhere unsafe. He wasn't sure why he doubted it, he just did.

From the looks of things, this was no regular clinic or hospital. Not even an urgent care center. The walls were made of stone, unlike anything he'd ever seen. Like something out of a medieval fairy tale, he mused before turning his attention back to the woman currently snacking on a bag of chips.

Where the hell were they, he wondered. And where could he get some of those salt and vinegar chips? Logan's stomach rumbled, and her head snapped up.

"Hungry? What do you want to eat?"

"Thanks, I am feeling a little peckish. Anything you have is fine, I don't want to put you out."

"Nonsense, the Keep loves preparing meals almost as much as Jessenia, our resident kitchen Wi-, er, chef," she said quickly, wiping her hands on a napkin that also seemed to appear out of thin air.

"Okay, how about a turkey sandwich?"

Logan was uncertain what else to say. Turkey was like universally safe, wasn't it? He watched her scamper out and wondered how long it would be till she returned. At least the redhead spoke to him, unlike the dude who was there earlier. That fucker seemed to hate him.

"Awesome. Be right back."

As the redhead left the room, barefoot and sighing happily, Logan got out of bed. His body ached in places he didn't even know he had, places he was sure had not been hit by his assailants. Harry, that fucker.

He had no idea what that man's problem was, but it wasn't good. He'd heard of corporate espionage and was always wary of folks inquiring into his research. But Harry had seemed harmless, and Logan told him nothing.

A wave of dizziness washed over Logan, and he held on to the bed, then the chair as he made his way over to a door that opened to reveal a bathroom. Just what he needed. Why hadn't he seen it there before?

After relieving himself he opted for a shower. Unsteady as he was, the railings proved useful as he turned the water on nice and hot and stood letting the spray hit him. Dirt and blood washed away as he soaped his body and shampooed his hair. Fuck, that felt good, but it was exhausting.

He exited the shower and took a fluffy towel from the shelf behind the toilet, wrapping it around his waist. Then he approached the mirror and found a toothbrush and paste.

As far as his life went, this was the most interesting series of days he'd had in a very long time. Let's see. First, he'd been picked up in a bar by the most beautiful and sexiest woman he had ever seen. He'd had the best sex of his life.

So great in fact was the sex, that after he'd woken up and found her gone, Logan had felt such intense heartbreak, he couldn't even begin to comprehend why. Now he knew. He'd somehow lost his heart to the beautiful Elena that very night.

Thinking of her didn't conjure the woman, but when he was in danger, she'd shown up. How and why, he had yet to answer. All he had to do was wait patiently for her to return, then he could do the first thing Logan had been dying to do since he'd seen her.

Okay. It was more like the second thing he'd been dying to do since he'd seen her. The first thing involved more of her and him naked. On the floor, against the wall, anywhere. He didn't care. He just wanted her.

Mind out of the gutter. Answers first, fucking later.

His dick softened as reason warred with primal desire. Logan shook his head. He needed to talk to Elena.

After he brushed his teeth, Logan took a good, long look at himself. He appeared no worse for wear. The one bruise visible on his temple had already taken on that yellow-gray hue that meant they were healing, and rapidly too. That was odd. He was sure he'd been hit on the head more than once, not to mention punched and kicked.

Alright. So, his ass had been handed to him. Yes, that was humiliating, but what interested him more was the fact he did not look like a guy whose ass had been handed to him.

How could he feel like he'd been hit by every car of a freight train, and not have a black eye? A fat lip? Any sort of *new* bruise or blemish?

The hair on the back of Logan's neck stood up and he reached around and touched it with his hand. Tiny electrical impulses seemed to dance up and down his spine and sweat dotted his brow. Frowning at the sudden, though not entirely unpleasant, assault on his system, he turned to see he was no longer alone.

She was there. His Elena. Though why he suddenly thought of her as his was worrisome.

Mine.

The thought invaded his brain, and he wasn't altogether sure it was his. Pulse racing, he realized he was staring at her. She was doing some looking of her own, and that alone gratified him as he turned to face her fully.

Elena stood in the doorway with a tray of food in her hands. She was so beautiful it almost hurt him to look at her.

What had he called her? A superhero? Goddess? Mystery woman? She was all those, and more. So much more.

Flesh and blood. Vivacious and striking. Tall and graceful. Her pink, bubble gum eyes flashed at him from across the room, and he felt her gaze rake over his body like hot coals. Everywhere they touched, those eyes seemed to leave trails of sizzling desire in their wake.

Especially, when they landed specifically on that part of him that had stood at attention the very moment Logan had felt her enter the room. Her eyes widened, and only then did he realize his towel had come loose.

"Shit," he muttered, reaching down for the bath sheet when a wave of dizziness washed over him.

How humiliating to wind up on the floor at her feet! Oh well, at least it was fitting. A woman like that should be worshipped. He could see her now with flowers and candles at her altar, being idolized by the mob.

No. Worshipped by me. Only me.

His thoughts turned jealous for a split second, catching him off guard. Another new for him. But he supposed that was to be expected, love being quite the emotion for a man whose last girlfriend had called him a man-sized brain wearing human skin.

It was love though. He recognized it as the truth soon as he saw her. Logan blinked rapidly, using both hands, palms flat on the tile floor, to stop his head from crashing into it.

Stupid towel. And now for the ultimate in humiliation, he thought and braced himself for impact. But before he hit ground, she was there, lifting him up with one arm around his waist, and the other gripping his right hand.

"Are you alright?" She asked, her husky voice sending shivers down his spine.

"I am now," Logan said, breathing in to inhale her subtle champagne rose scent.

It was too late to stop the lame words from passing his lips. Shit. He sounded like some lovesick asshole. But still, his body was weak from whatever had happened. So, he took her help gratefully.

Logan wasn't exactly driven by testosterone. He had no problem with strong women, and she was fierce, his Elena. He wanted to just stay there with her in comfortable silence, to bask in the warmth of her heated blush colored gaze, but he needed answers.

"Here, let's get you back in bed," she murmured, her cheeks burning pink, much like the warm glow of her stare.

Disregarding the towel, Elena helped him back to the bed, tossing the sheet over his waist, and trying to act nonchalant about it. But Logan knew better. He'd seen that telltale blush cross her perfect face, and he had to bite the inside of his mouth to stop from grinning.

At least I didn't imagine her attraction to me.

Point one for Logan.

"Uh, I brought you food," Elena said, pushing the cart holding a tray laden with more food than he could ever eat closer to him.

He took the bottle of water first and drank half of it before he spoke again. Fuck, that felt good against his dry throat. His stomach growled, and he realized he was, in fact hungry.

Elena had turned to leave, but he was so not having that. No way. He never wanted her to move out of his sight.

Baby steps, he reminded himself.

"Wait," he said, gasping for air after such a long pull from the bottle. "Please, I need answers."

"Okay," she turned, and nodded. "Ask me anything."

His head swam with things he wanted to know. Like where did she get those crazy beautiful bubble gum eyes? Why did she leave him the other night? And could he kiss her again and maybe never stop?

But Logan was a scientist. There were other things he needed to know first. He just couldn't think of them right now. And that was another first. How could one woman render his brain so utterly void of coherent thought?

"Well, I'm sure you want to know who those men were who attacked you?" Elena began.

Her eyebrows raised, and he realized they were not platinum like her hair, but black, and from what he could see, totally natural. As was the rest of her. She wore no makeup, needed no embellishments.

Her eyes were unbelievably pretty, and a color he'd never seen in nature. Not the red of albinism, or the blue violet of Liz Taylor, but pink. True, bubble gum pink.

His cock went hard again, and he was thankful for the sheet he had draped over himself once again. Logan swallowed another sip of cool water. He felt warm all over. Needy, antsy, and restless too. But he pushed back those base feelings and lasered a stare at her.

"Actually," he began, his voice deep and low. "I wanted to know why you left the other night after what was probably the best sex I'd ever had in my entire life."

Chapter Ten

Elena's face burned with embarrassment. Not only was she fighting her desire to jump him. And boy, did she really want to. Her lips tingled with the need to kiss him. Her mouth salivated as she imagined licking every beautiful, exposed inch of him. The last thing she needed to do was give every listening ear a special show.

Grrr.

When she did kiss him. If he wanted to, that was. It would not be with an audience. She stopped her growling. So, what if he'd just pretty much announced they'd fucked to a house full of supernaturals. Three of whom were just outside the door. It wasn't like they didn't already know.

Shit. Shit. SHIT.

"Uh, well, that is, uh," Elena tried, but found she couldn't really answer him.

What could she say that would even make sense to him? Let alone make up for what she'd done.

Sorry, I was embarrassed after I went into my heat, saw you, and couldn't keep my hands off you?

Wait. Did he say the *best sex* of his life? Warmth filled her and Elena could not stop the grin from spreading across her face. Even better was the return smile he gifted her with. A thousand watts of unadulterated male hotness, and it was all aimed at her. Just for her. The knowledge made her inner kitty purr.

Prrr.

Kingston walked in before she could say anything else. Good. At least the big fucker wasn't just lurking in the hallway anymore. Holley was with him, and so was Fergie, who inched her way over to where she'd dropped her shoes and bag. The she-Wolf hated going barefoot

"Excuse me, folks, gotta run," she said, then winked at Elena, who really wanted to just disappear at that moment.

"Hello. You're Logan?" Kingston addressed the normal, his voice booming with power. "Are you well enough to talk?"

"I think so yes, I was just dizzy before---"

"Dizzy? Hang on a moment," Holley said, moving towards the table where she'd left tiny bottles of potions.

"Here," she said, handing him a vial. "Drink this, it will help you fight off the poison."

"What poison? And what is this?" Logan said, eyebrows furrowed.

His handsome face paled, and Elena rushed to his side before he could tip off the bed. Something was wrong. He was not responding to the antidotes as well as they'd expected.

"You must drink that vial, Logan," Holley repeated.

He looked up, hazel eyes boring into Elena's, and she saw the question there. She nodded her head, encouragingly. Hardly expecting him to trust her, but needing him well, Elena implored him to drink it.

"We are here to help you, Logan. I swear it. And I promise, I will answer every question you have, but please, drink the vial first."

He looked at her with a serious mien, hazel eyes capturing her expression, and validating her veracity. It was like she could see the wheels in his head turning as he weighed his options and her sincerity.

"I want you to know," he said, speaking to her. "This is difficult for me. Taking a drug without knowing what it is, but if you trust her," he nodded to Elena, and a wave of humility washed over her, as she nodded.

"I do, Logan. I trust Holley."

"Then, I will drink it."

That he put his faith in her, trusted her with this decision, was momentous. He was a full human. Logan Wells knew nothing of their world, and yet, something inside told him he could rely on her.

Joy filled her. Pure happiness that made her glow with warmth as he took her hand in his, long fingers, easily capturing hers, and tossed the vial back. Elena's Panther purred, the feline proud that her mate was allowing her to take care of him.

We can't know for certain that he is our mate. Not yet, she told the beast.

Her kitty hissed at the thought, but went back to purring when she looked at Logan's handsome face. He really was good looking. Chiseled features, even a small cleft in his chin. He had plump lips that she knew to be talented. Long and lean, with just the right amount of muscle, she still remembered the feel of his strong body against hers.

"Alright?" she asked, waiting as he sat eyes closed while the potion took effect.

"Better?" Holley asked, grinning widely when his eyebrows raised, and he nodded his assent.

"Yes. I'd love to study that sometime," he said.

"Study it? Do musicians do that?" Elena asked.

"Oh, uh," he blushed and rubbed the back of his neck in that adorable manner that had her practically panting.

"I'm only a musician on Thursdays," he replied.

"Come again?" she asked.

"Actually, I'm a scientist. A geneticist and biochemist. My work is to try and uncover the origins of certain disease, birth defects and the like, and then in turn to develop ways to prevent or treat them using what I can learn from specific genes. I try to answer why certain people react specifically to certain stimuli like chemical and environmental reactions."

"I see," Elena murmured.

"Who do you work for now?" Kingston asked.

"Myself, mostly. I used to work for a pharmaceutical company but found out too late they were not as interested in helping people as they were in selling medicine to them at exorbitant prices. I left and was forced to sign an NDA."

"And you've continued this work on your own?" she asked, curiosity piqued.

Elena had no idea the man she'd been so undeniably attracted to had a big brain along with his killer bod. Maybe that had something to do with the Loyalists wanting him? She'd have to run the idea past Kingston, though one look at the Dragon told her he'd reached the same conclusion.

"Not that work, per se, but I have been trying to identify what makes some people resilient to certain diseases and injuries. For example, I recently stumbled upon a blood sample of a man who'd been in an explosion in a warehouse that should have left him dead. The man was found barely alive days later and survived his injuries far longer than any normal human being should have," Logan explained, shaking his head.

"He succumbed eventually, but not before contacts of mine got me some samples. But they must have been tainted."

"Tainted?" Kingston asked, his Dragon peeking out through his eyes.

Elena moved closer to Logan. Kingston was her Alpha, and she trusted him. But she felt an overwhelming sense of possessiveness about the human male, and her protective instincts were going berserk.

Whether she was ready to admit it or not, the man obviously meant a lot to her.

"So, the men who attacked you were there because of something having to do with your work? With this tainted sample?" Holley asked, obviously trying to lighten the tension between the Dragon and Elena.

"I don't see how, but maybe," Logan shrugged.

Elena was learning so many new things about the man she'd let fuck her stupid, she froze in place. Like she'd turned to stone as a million and one doubts came at her from all angles.

He was smart. Really smart. What would he see in her? She passed school, barely. Her dad had spent all his time training her to fight. Elena liked martial arts, and hard rock, and horror films. What did she have that could possibly interest him?

"Hey, are you okay?"

His hazel gaze found hers, and he seemed to trace every inch of her face like those strong, long fingered hands had done not too long ago. Her body came alive under that stare. Warming and swelling in places she'd never felt before.

"Do you need water or something?"

She shook her head. Elena was positively speech-less. He had that effect on her. He was all beautiful male, and smart as hell, too. She didn't stand a chance.

It was part of the reason she always paired up with Byram or even Egros. They were both incredibly smart, and where she found conversations with them stimulating, she partnered with them for her superior ability to kick ass.

Storm, Furio, and Kingston, were all fairly intelligent. But Shifters tended to run on instinct and physical dominance. She did not partner with them as often for the simple reason that they stunted her in battle.

As a female Shifter, they could not help but want to protect and shelter her. But she wasn't some weak woman they needed to baby. She was fierce. A motherfucking warrior in her own right.

Elena had taken to pairing with either the Vampire or the Witch when on assignment. Neither tried to shelter her or sacrifice themselves for her. They allowed her to excel at what she did. And she was a good Guardian. She knew that without being told.

Of course, with her recent heat cycle, everything had changed. She thought sadly of Egros. She'd hurt the male Witch by turning down his offer to see her through her heat, but what could she say? She was simply not interested in him in that way. But that was a problem for another day.

Elena turned back to Logan. He was watching, waiting patiently for her attention. When she nodded, he seemed to expel the breath he was holding. Then he turned to answer Holley.

"The man who seemed to lead the attack was a guy named Harry. He's a frequent customer at *Midnight's*, or at least from what I saw of him on Thursdays for the past five months or so since I've been playing there."

"I see," Kingston said, encouraging him to go on.

"He was insistent that I speak to him about my current research, but it makes no sense. The sample from that warehouse victim was tainted."

"Why do you think it was tainted?" Holley inquired.

"Because what I saw in that man's blood is humanly impossible," Logan replied.

"Where was the warehouse?' Elena asked, a terrible dread filling her stomach.

Kingston stared at her as Logan repeated the address, and Elena felt the walls closing in. Fuck. That warehouse was where the Guardians had battled a group of Gila Shifter Loyalists a few weeks back. There'd been no actual explosion, merely a good dousing of *Dragonfire*.

Typically, that would incinerate all evidence of supernatural battles, including corpses. Somehow, they must have missed one of the Loyalists. He probably hid somewhere in the bowels of the warehouse while Kingston unleashed his fire.

Dammit.

Elena had been there. But not alone. That was the thing about the Guardians. They worked together, and not one of them ever took the blame for a mission failed.

It was team work all around. But this was an epic fuck up. Their failure led to a human finding genetic proof of the supernatural. And that was unacceptable.

"I can tell by your faces, that I've uncovered something big, something secret," Logan began, and Kingston bared his teeth at him.

"Stop Kingston," Elena growled and moved to turn to face her Alpha, but Logan refused to release her hand.

"Before you try to threaten or lie to me, I have a question. Which one of you is the Dragon?"

At that insolent remark, Kingston roared, and Elena leaned over. Closer still to the man, who was increasingly important to her. She wasn't sure what she would do if Kingston attacked.

Well, that wasn't true. She was surprisingly very certain of what she would do in that instance. Elena was simply having difficulty accepting it.

Mine.

"What do you know of Dragons?" Kingston demanded.

"You will back away from him," Elena snarled.

After that, all hell broke loose. Before Kingston could attack, Elena leapt onto the foot of the bed, putting herself between the Dragon and the scientist.

Body trembling in rage at the threat to her mate, Elena could hardly think, let alone contain her beast. She shifted from human to Panther in the blink of an eye, stunning all there. Especially Logan.

"Holy fucking shit," he whispered, and she felt more than saw his wide eyed stare on her black furry back while she faced off her Alpha. The Diamond Dragon was not pleased. Smoke puffed from his nostrils, but Elena's Panther hissed and snarled, spitting angry at the male for baring his fangs at her mate.

Thank the gods for Holley. She was faster, and smarter than them all, she wove a spell that slammed into Logan, sending him to sleep while she pushed her mate out into the hallway.

After a furiously whispered conversation, Kingston beckoned Elena.

"Shift, dress, then my office. Now. I'll call the others," Kingston snarled angrily.

"It is okay, El. I will watch over him. He will sleep for some time now."

Holley turned spreading her arms wide and gestured for her to follow Kingston. Well, fuck. This was one shitshow she really didn't want to be a part of but what choice did she have?

"Traitor."

"I don't believe it."

"She told her lover all about us!"

"How could you think that?"

"It doesn't matter now."

On and on, the arguing went until Elena was wiped out emotionally. Byram was absent, out on assignment. Egros thought she'd betrayed them. Furio and Storm were staunchly in her corner, prepared to defend her against any and all.

While Elena appreciated the gesture, she did not need them to defend her. She'd done nothing wrong. At least, not anything that could have jeopardized them.

"I can't believe I have to say this, but I have not betrayed our secret," Elena stated to the group once the yelling stopped.

"El," Storm, her staunchest supporter so far, started, but she cut him off.

Anger and disbelief warred with the desire to simply walk out on them and go to her mate's side. But she knew she would never feel anything even close to peace if she did that now. Too many things left unsaid were bad for the soul.

"I took my vows as a Guardian of Chaos before some of you here. I have given my life to our cause, to keep magic free for all beings. You are the closest I have to family since my mother died, and my father all but disowned me---"

"And yet, you let your heat cycle control your behavior! You put us all in violation of the Assembly's strict guidelines just because you wanted to fuck a human. You put us in danger to satisfy your urges. How could you, Elena?"

Egros' growled words were like a slap to the face. She stepped back, shocked. Storm growled and yelled at the Witch, causing Furio to step between them. Then she did something she'd never thought herself capable of. She tossed her head back and roared with all the power of her beast, silencing all the voices in the room.

"You bastard," she stated quietly, more pissed off than ever before.

"How dare you be so dismissive of something you know nothing about? You are a Witch, not a Shifter. You have no idea what a heat cycle is or does to a woman."

"El, I don't think he meant---"

"I know what he meant, Storm. He's angry I turned him down when he offered to spend my heat with me. And now, he wants to try to shame me for it."

The hush that fell over them was thick and ominous. But she was done being a punching bag for the Witch. Sometimes feelings got hurt in the course of one's life. It was a bitch, but it happened, and she was finished with being blamed for not wanting him back.

"Alright, that's enough now," Kingston said.

"Is it? I am sick and tired of you males telling me what to do or weighing in on something you cannot possibly understand. Only Furio and Storm know better! Wolves and Mares in heat are nothing to joke about. Right, boys? Dragons either, I assume."

"El---"

"No, Egros is right about one thing. My heat cycle is not something I can always control, and that sucks, but who I chose to satisfy that biological urge with is no one's business but mine! I am every bit the warrior I always was, and I am loyal to the Guardians."

"Point taken. But you must admit this is more than that, Elena. You came between me and the human," Kingston asked with something close to pride on his face.

"I did that because," she said, flushing, but it was more than past time she confessed the truth. Elena turned towards her Alpha and cleared her throat.

"My Panther is pretty sure Logan is mine."

Her inner kitty purred in delight that she had voiced the words, and Elena stood tall, ignoring the hooting gasps from some in the room. Whatever happened, she needed Kingston to know where she stood. Everything inside her was pointing her firmly in the direction of the sole human inside the Keep.

Logan Wells. My fated mate.

Mine.

Prrrr.

Chapter Eleven

*F*uck.

Logan blinked, head pounding as he slowly came awake. What the fuck had happened this time?

Memories flooded his somewhat addled brain, and then he knew. Perhaps he should've been a bit more tactful about the whole witnessing a Dragon thing?

"Ya think?" Someone said.

He sat up too quickly, holding his head and scanning the room until his eyes landed on two men. One had electric blue eyes, the other long hair, and a mulish expression. They were somewhat familiar, but he couldn't place either.

"Yo cump. So, you and El? Treat her right, you feel me," blue eyes said.

"Uh," eyebrows raised, Logan did not respond.

"Easy dude, we're just, you know, like her big *bruthas.*"

"I see," Logan said, clearing his throat.

"She ain't like other girls. None of us are, but you know that, right?"

"You guys turn into, uh, Panthers too?" He squeaked.

"No offense, but I ain't no pussy, bro," blue eyes snarled, and something about him screamed canine. Maybe he could turn into a German Shepherd or something?

"Okay, sorry. I, um, that is, *where* is Elena?" Logan inquired, feeling antsy under the hardened stare of both men.

There was something positively feral in their gazes, even though they were not being overly threatening. Not a pussy, huh? Logan wondered then what he could be. A Wolf or a Bear. If people could turn into Dragons and Panthers, why not other creatures as well.

The possibilities sent his mind racing. Holy shit. Questions burned his brain. About them, this place.

The way the room seemed to change at whim, his or whoever entered.

Where is she?

He felt needy, restless. One night with Elena, and he was hooked. Every time he thought of her his dick got hard, and his mouth went dry. Dammit. She showed no sign of wanting him again.

Despite his feelings, and as for those, what was he wearing a sign or something? These two fuckers could tell exactly what he'd been thinking if their smirks were anything to go by.

"Why you wanna know, cump? Miss her already?"

Yeah. He definitely had a sign on his forehead. A bright fucking pink neon one that he was pretty sure said something like '*Caution: Idiot prone to falling in love with one night stands way out of his league*' or something like it.

Either way, he had enough of these two guys. And he had no intention of divulging anything to either of them.

"Look, just tell me where she is---"

"Why should we?"

"Because I need to talk to her."

The long haired placed a big hand on blue eyes, and the latter stopped glaring. That was something at least. Logan was not intimidated, not really. And that surprised the fuck out of him.

"She'll be along soon. You know, we hear you're a scientist?"

"Yes, I am."

"You know anything about botany?"

"Um, a little, why?"

"My ma-, *er*, wife is having a hard time with her indoor herbal garden. Something is wonky with her plants. Every time she introduces anything new to the soil, fertilizer, soft water, anything really, it seems to wipe out the thyme, but not the others," the man said and pulled his long hair back from his face, arranging it in a low ponytail that the other guy pulled.

Shit. Did he just whinny? What the fuck was going on here? Logan nodded to get the man's attention.

"Thyme? Uh, sounds like she needs to introduce some diversity in the genetic makeup of the plant. Maybe by introducing different varieties in the same patch, she could crossbreed and create a sturdier plant?"

"Diversity, huh? Okay, Doc. I'll tell her."

"Doc?"

"You're a doctor, right?"

"I have doctorates," he shrugged.

"Cool. I'm Furio, this here is Storm. We'll be seeing you, Doc."

The two men nodded and walked out, and for a moment he wondered if he was going to be alone long enough to get dressed to try to find Elena. But just like that, she returned.

Logan's gaze roamed over her from head to toe. She looked different here. In worn jeans and a tank top that did nothing to hide her subtle curves and elegant physique to his hungry eyes.

Fuck, he really loved looking at her. She was like a sculpture or painting made by masters. Even better because Elena was flesh and blood. So warm and lively, beautiful in an understated way that belied her power and lethality.

"Feeling better?" She asked, and her small tongue darted out to wet her lips.

"You mean after your friend knocked me out?" He softened the remark with a smile the second he saw her face fall.

Logan was such a prick sometimes. And he really didn't want to be. Not with her. She deserved better than that and he wanted to be better to her. *For her.* She didn't need his attitude.

"I'm sorry," he began.

"Why are you sorry?"

"For being nasty. I didn't mean it."

"Are you kidding? Let's see, I basically attacked you the other night in the club. Ran out on you the next day without a word. Show up a week later without warning. Almost get you killed. Then I kidnapped you. Turned into a Panther in front of you---"

"Actually, I am pretty sure you saved my life," he interrupted.

Nerves on edge, he felt tongue tied and his stomach was in knots. Logan was breathing like a marathon runner as he watched her. He felt things he hadn't since he was a kid talking to his first hot girl.

"I'm glad you came back. To the club, I mean. I have questions of course."

"Logan, there's only so much I can tell you," she replied, biting her lip in a gesture he found both endearing and maddening.

She was so strong and fierce, but when her bubble gum eyes glanced his way, he saw untold vulnerability and that made his heart ache for her. Without thinking, he held out his hand, thrilled when she took it, allowing him to pull her close.

Elena sat on the bed, facing him, her hip

brushing his. Even through the sheet, the contact sent tendrils of awareness coursing through his blood. Logan had never had such an intense physical reaction to a woman. Even if she was so more than that, so much more than what she seemed.

"Logan," she whispered his name, raising a hand to caress his cheek.

He closed his eyes, reveling at the contact, and pressed his face firmly into her palm. Fuck, that felt good. He wanted more, need more of her. Without any thought beyond that, he reached for her.

Logan pressed his mouth to hers. At first, he touched his lips to hers softly, tenderly, then with a deep, fervent desire he simply could not deny. Logan wanted her more than he wanted air to breathe.

Every inch of him was acutely attuned to Elena. To the way she moaned into his mouth, the increased frequency of her breathing, and the unsteady pounding of her heart against his. He squeezed her tightly to his chest, loving the way she molded to him.

Usually, Logan was too tall, too big for his women, but she was a perfect match. Her tall, svelte body melted into him, and he tightened his hold, dipping her head back until it rested on his arm while he plundered her mouth greedily.

She tasted like bubble gum, champagne, and roses. Like toasted marshmallows, cayenne pepper, and desire.

"Elena," he moaned her name, disbelieving she was there, real and in his arms.

Logan's cock was so damn hard he thought he was going to burst. Need and desire warred with each other as their kiss went on and on and on. And still, it wasn't enough.

He could go on kissing her forever. Despite the growing ache in his balls and the throbbing of his dick. Just holding her and kissing her for as long as he could. That alone was the culmination of every fantasy he'd ever had.

No one ever made him feel this way. Logan had thought himself in love a time or two, but no woman had ever owned him so completely. And Elena owned him, alright. Could make him her slave if she wanted to.

The real question was, did she want too? Did she want him?

"I do want you," she whispered, slowing their kiss, and leaving them both panting and shivering with unsatisfied need.

"But we need to talk."

"I'm listening, but stay here, okay? Don't move,"

he begged, dropping another soft kiss to her sweet, swollen lips.

"Okay," she murmured.

And that was how she came to tell him about all the magnificent, wonderful, impossible things she and her group of Guardians were while draped across his lap in bed in a place he learned was called the Keep, a magical fortress whose only mission was to protect and serve the Guardians who dwelled within.

It was a lot for Logan to take in. Almost too much. But then he started adding things together. What other explanation could there be?

"So, you are a Guardian of Chaos? Why chaos?"

"We protect magic in its most pure form," she explained. "From chaos comes creation, and magic is unfortunately, finite in this realm. It is needed by all supernaturals, and even normals though they don't realize it. Our biggest enemy is a group called the Loyalists. Their endgame is to control all magic, to siphon it out as they see fit. We are sworn to stop them."

"I see. I mean, I'm trying to see. It is all quite fascinating," he said, trying to wrap his mind around it.

"You think that Harry and his men are part of them, the Loyalists?"

"We know they are," she replied.

"And they wanted me because why exactly?"

"We think you learned something you weren't supposed to when you got that sample from the warehouse victim, though I would not call him that," she hedged.

"What do you mean?"

"I think you found a Loyalist, most likely a Gila Shifter, who'd been hiding from us in the warehouse. Somehow, he went undetected and when Kingston used his *Dragonfire* to cleanse the place, he survived."

"So, you guys burnt a man to death?"

"Not a man, and not on purpose," she started defensively.

"Easy, sweetheart, I didn't mean to sound judgmental. If the bastard was fighting against you, he deserved what he got," Logan stated, and unsurprisingly, he meant every word of it.

"Vicious thing," she grinned, and kissed his mouth hungrily.

Passion exploded as he wrapped her up in his arms. He had the feeling she was holding back with him, careful to not break him, but Logan somehow knew that there was nothing she would do to hurt him

And there it was again. That word whispered into his brain.

Mine.

He wanted to say it aloud. To yell it from the rooftops. Hell, Logan wanted to tell her she belonged to him and he to her. Like some barbaric caveman, for fuck's sake. And just the thought of tossing her sweet ass over his shoulder and bringing her back to his den so he could stamp himself all over her fine body sounded really fucking good.

His thoughts shocked him, but that didn't stop his dick from throbbing with need. He fought himself, hoping his rational mind would resume control of his body and brain.

Easy. She's a person not a blow up doll. Sex was great, but it needed to wait. Logan was not going to allow his base needs to disrupt or fuck with what could very well be the love of his life. For now, he would have to be content with discussion.

"So, magic is real," he said, waiting for her nod to continue.

"And you protect it."

"Yes."

"And it exists in a finite quantity, recycling itself to those who use it? Supernaturals?"

"Yes and no. The human world uses magic too, it's just not as aware of it as we are."

"I see, too many scientists among us." He grinned sheepishly.

"Oh no, there is nothing wrong with science. I find chemical reactions fascinating," she replied, and fuck him, his cock went hard again.

"You do?"

"Uh huh. Science, magic, it all blends once you know what to look for. You know, Logan, I am really interested in that mind of yours."

"You are?"

"Yes. Does that surprise you?" She whispered, and he saw through to the vulnerability he knew she kept hidden from the rest of the world.

"That you'd be interested in science? No. That you'd be interested in me. A little, yes."

"That's the thing about Shifters," she explained. "We know when we like someone."

"And you like me?"

"I like you."

Logan's heart soared at the words. She liked him. The beautiful, magical, powerful, and sexy as hell creature liked him. Like *liked* him.

As if that wasn't thrilling enough, it was like the pieces of his life and career as a scientist were all falling into place. Every suspicion he'd ever had, as both man and back when he was a child, seemed true.

He'd always thought there was more out there than the humans controlling the world seemed ready to share with the rest of society. More to it than global warming and the effects of nuclear warfare.

"Those things are very real though," Elena pointed out, and he smiled and kissed her again.

"Yes, but so are Dragons and Witches. And, hey, what are you exactly?"

But before she could reply, Furio and Storm interrupted with a knock.

"Yo, El, we gotta run. The sensors we left at Doc's are going haywire. Someone tripped them."

"Shit," she muttered, and leapt off his lap.

"Wait. Doc is me, right?"

Her cheeks burned pink, but she nodded and slipped her shoes back on her feet. He wasn't sure when she'd kicked those off. But it occurred to him she was going to walk into danger in his house. For him.

Hell fucking no. She wasn't leaving him behind. No way, no how.

"I'm coming too."

Logan stood up, clutching the sheet.

"No," she said, shaking her pretty little head.

"Yes, I am. There are things I need from the lab in my house you won't be able to get to without me. Biometrics," he said wiggling his fingers, and wagging his eyebrows.

"Fuck. Look, it might be dangerous."

"Then I guess you'll just have to protect me, *kitten.*"

The nick name just sorta came out, and Logan waited to see if she objected. She didn't say anything, so he stood and looked for clothes. Her silence disturbing, he turned and saw Elena's mouth wide open.

A wicked grin crossed his face and Logan had to admit, he was mighty pleased by her reaction to his nudity. Looked like his kitten liked what she saw if the deep purring sound she made in the back of her throat was any indication.

He took the folded pair of jeans and sweatshirt that someone had left and shrugged into them, taking his time. He liked knowing her bubble gum gaze was riveted to the lines of his body. Was proud of his thick, hard cock, liked her knowing she did that to him. Logan opted for no socks as he stepped into his worn sneakers, finally turning to face her.

"So, what are you exactly? *Panthera pardus or panthera onca?*" Logan asked as the four of them huddled into a souped up Jeep Wrangler that Storm was driving.

"Neither. I am not some cat you find in the zoo," she snorted derisively, and he laughed.

She looked exactly like his grandfather's haughty old house cat when she wore that expression. Head raised, eyes forward, so regal and confident in her beauty.

"Well?"

"*I* am a Black Panther. I have no true wild cousins. My line is strictly supernatural, but we are the inspiration for the *Panther Incensed*. You're probably familiar-"

"My tattoo," Logan grinned. "My grandfather is descended from England. He showed me our family crest once and the *Panther Incensed* was right there in black and gold."

"Is that why?"

"Yeah, sort of. The panther is part of Wells family history. I always felt drawn to it," he murmured, eyes roaming over her fair skin and brilliant eyes.

In the din of the vehicle, Elena was all silver moonlight and pink bubble gum eyes, scenting of roses and champagne. Like a beautiful dream he could not have imagined, even if he had tried with all his might.

An ethereal vision he would never forget. Like her image was forever burned in his brain, stamped there, tattooed just like the *Panther Incensed* on his side.

"We playing twenty questions here? Pay attention, Doc. This could get dangerous," Furio warned as they pulled up to his townhouse faster than he could have imagined.

"Magic?" he asked, and Elena winked and nodded.

Damn. She was so fucking gorgeous. His cock twitched, despite it being anything but the right time for such a reaction. He couldn't help it, and even if he could, he wouldn't. Elena made him feel things he'd never felt before.

He felt virile, alive, and all fucking man. Especially when she looked at him with those crazy gorgeous eyes of hers. Right now they were glowing, and he grabbed her hand, squeezing tight before Storm parked the car, and they all jumped out.

"Stay where they can see you, I am going around

back to make sure it's clear," she instructed, all business as she cased the street.

He nodded, having no intention of putting himself or her in harm's way. Logan was a scientist, that meant he was not only practical, he was also logical and methodical. He was certainly man enough to accept the fact that she was the warrior here, not him.

"No playin' hero, Doc," Furio seconded after Elena's pert ass disappeared around the corner.

Holy hell.

She was so fucking hot when she was being all superhero stealthy. Again with his dick getting hard at inappropriate times, he shrugged and pinched himself nonchalantly. Fuck, he couldn't help it though.

She was like a comic book sex kitten superhero beauty queen. His dream woman in real life with her skinny jeans outlining long, powerful legs and firm backside.

Her breasts were high and snug in the tight tank she wore, giving the most alluring hint of cleavage. A nerd's wet dream, for sure. She was Logan's every secret fantasy come to life.

"No worries," Logan replied when he caught Furio still watching him. "You three are the

Guardians. I'm just a regular guy. I don't need to grab a ruler or anything."

"What?" Furio asked, cocking his head to the side.

"He means he doesn't need no dick measuring contest to see which of us is the man," Storm translated.

"Damn fucking straight, Doc," Furio nodded.

"Afraid you'd lose, horse face?" snorted Storm.

"Fuck you, Pound Puppy."

Their insults were not entirely lost on him, Logan just shook his head and jogged behind Storm as they headed for his front door. The wind whipped through the borrowed sweatshirt he wore, and he was freezing.

Logan didn't know how the three of them did it with tanks and tees, but he was grateful they'd be heading back inside. February was a cold bitch.

Storm leaned forward, sniffing the front door loudly before nodding his head and waving them forward. Logan wondered where his kitten had gone off to. Before he could worry, relief filled him as her scent reached his nostrils.

"Whoever was here, they're long gone," Elena told the three men from her position stretched out on top of the large hutch in the dining room, reminding Logan of his grandfather's old Russian blue.

That cat was a real beauty, with tons of arrogance bred into him through his prestigious lineage. But Duke the Cat had nothing on her. His own living breathing *Panther Incensed*.

Grandfather would be so proud, he mused. He wondered briefly what Margo would say.

"Took you guys long enough." Elena winked before jumping down, landing on her feet gracefully.

Just like a kitty, he thought. Furio and Storm checked the other rooms to be sure, and Elena stalked across towards him. She leaned close as she passed, rubbing her cheek against his, and touching his chest and back.

"Where does this door go?" she asked, pointing to the entry to the basement where he'd set up his lab.

That door had obviously been busted, with what looked like claw marks and other signs of damage. Fuck. It looked like a rabid dinosaur had attacked his home. Logan followed Elena down the stairs, into the normal looking basement, to the second door.

"Shit got ugly here," Storm said, taking in the damage that had been inflicted on logan's security door.

Unlucky for whoever was trying to bust in, but good for Logan, the culprits had failed in their attempt. His biometric security system had been activated by the intruders. Judging from the angry scratches against the door and the broken mechanical arm hanging from just above the portal, the pepper spray he'd set up to keep out unlawful snoops had been deployed.

"You used mace?" Elena grinned, pointing to the empty can that was still held by the robotic arm.

"Pepper spray. It was designed to be activated in the event of a break in," he shrugged then proceeded to scan his fingerprints, type in his secret code, and lastly, the optical scan.

"Wow, this is really something," Elena looked around his laboratory, and he felt his chest swell with pride.

"Thanks," he shrugged. "Here. These are the reports I have on the sample I took."

"Okay, let's take that and anything else you think you might need to replicate whatever it was you were doing that the Loyalists might want. Do you mind doing that? I mean, we could stay here---"

"No, I think it's better we go. This place has obviously been breached."

"I am so sorry, Logan---"

"It's just stuff, sweetheart. It can be replaced. Come help me," he said, turning to gather equipment.

Elena seemed pleased he'd asked her and worked side by side with him, following his instruction to the letter. Furio and Storm kept guard, occasionally coming down to carry out a crate or two. After an hour, they'd assembled most of his files and equipment for transport to the Keep.

"I'd like to stop by *Midnight's* to get my bass," Logan said after they'd all filed back into the Jeep.

"Oh no! I meant to grab it, but I guess I got side-tracked---" Elena confessed, and her cheeks burned the same pretty color as her eyes.

"You mean with saving my life and all? No worries, sweetheart. I don't need it," Logan murmured, but it was what he'd left unsaid that really mattered.

I need you.

Chapter Twelve

Midnight's was closed to the public when they arrived, and Elena had a terrible feeling in the pit of her stomach.

"You guys keep watch, okay? I'm going to go with him."

"Sure, El," Storm said, nodding his head.

"Come on, we can go through the back," Logan said, motioning her forward.

Elena could have kicked herself for forgetting his bass the other night, but she was more worried about saving his life and all. On high alert, she followed behind her mate while he attempted to retrieve his instrument.

"That's weird," he murmured when he reached the back door.

A delivery truck blocked the far end of the alley, and Elena could not see Furio or Storm from where they were standing. The feeling of impending danger grew.

"Come on. We should go."

"What? Why? Let me just check the door," Logan said, and reached for the handle.

Then everything moved really fast. The door blew open from the inside and three half-shifted Gila monsters leapt out to grab Logan. Her mate turned around quickly, his face one of shock and horror.

"Elena, run!" He screamed at her, trying to use his own body to guard her from harm.

Sweet mate. Kill those fuckers.

Her Panther snarled, and Elena didn't hesitate to shift. She tossed her head back and roared, knowing full well Storm and Furio would hear her.

"Got you now," the man called Harry said as he cuffed Logan in shackles and started to pull him down the alley towards the van.

"Kill that bitch, then meet me at the base," he commanded his men, but something happened before he could utter another word.

Harry's hands went to his neck, and Elena saw

Logan had looped the chain from his shackles around the man's throat.

"I got him," Logan yelled. "Watch out behind you!"

Realizing her mate was taking care of himself, she turned to meet the two Gila bastards who were attempting to spit at her with their venomous saliva. It was the one thing the bastards had over the Guardians. Their deadliest weapon, indeed.

But Elena was fast. Faster than ever before. She dodged a spit attack from one then two as Furio charged a third down in his fiery Pegasus skin. Storm battled another with blue rays of energy adding power to his punches. The Guardians were holding their own.

She turned when she heard Logan scream, Harry had stomped backwards on his foot and was even now trying to free himself. But her wiry mate was relentless. Even falling on the floor he pulled hard against the Shifter's shackles, choking him till he was immobilized.

Elena roared and suddenly pink flames shot from her mouth. She glanced at the door to Midnight's and caught sight of her reflection.

Holy fuck.

She had iridescent pink flames sparking at her fingertips, ears, mouth, even her hair! She felt powerful and furious. Ready to defend her mate with her newly increased magic.

Mine, her inner kitty roared, enraged at the bastards who thought it was okay to touch him.

She really was a *Panther Incensed.* The only time she'd seen a panther roaring flames out of its mouth was in heraldic images like Logan's tattoo. And what could have her more incensed than her mate in danger.

More Gila Shifters filed into the alley, but they did not stand a chance. Not against Storm, Furio, and Logan. And certainly not against her.

Roar.

* * *

After the battle was over, Kingston arrived with some local Enforcers. Together, they arrested and interrogated the prisoners before transporting them far away from human civilization.

"As far as people will know, there was a gas leak here and the street will be evacuated for a few hours

while we clean up," Elena had explained on the way back to the Keep.

She'd been worried Logan would want to go back to his place. To be free to move on with his life and to get out of hers. The very idea filled her with dread. But he hadn't said anything of the sort, merely slid into the car, and when she sat next to him, he'd twined his long fingers with hers.

They were all safe for now. And what's more, he'd come back home with her. She would just have to be happy with that, she thought as she walked back to the car.

"You can't keep him, you know," Egros' voice had Elena spinning around to face him as she helped unload the Jeep with Logan's things.

"What?"

"He's human, El," the Witch spat. "He doesn't belong here. You shouldn't have told him about us. There are rules---"

"Egros, we both know why you are saying these things. I thought you were my friend," Elena said, her voice cracking with the thought of decades of friendship being tossed away.

"I am your friend," the male Witch yelled hoarsely, tossing a ball of energy into the far wall that left a big burnt spot in the stone.

Egros looked defeated, angry, defiant even. Not like someone she trusted or recognized. Not like the Guardian she had fought alongside of for so long. What was happening to them? She wanted to yell at him, but Elena also didn't want to explain herself to him. She shouldn't have to.

"I am your friend," he said with slightly more control. "The Assembly is convening. They will decide if he needs to be bespelled to forget-"

"What? You called the Assembly? How dare you!" Elena raged, but before she could attack him. Storm, Jessenia, and Logan arrived.

"I did it for you!" Egros yelled, but Storm was blocking the Witch.

"What's going on here? What did he do to you?" Logan asked, gaze locking with the seething male Witch in the corner being held back by Storm.

"What did *I* do? *You* are at fault here! Puny normal, you've ruined her! How can she have a future with someone so utterly beneath her on the evolutionary scale? You were supposed to be for one night! Just a nothing of a coupling to help her through her heat! Not her mate! Not her fucking fated mate! She can't even know for sure if her hormones are still whacked. How can she even think that you are hers?"

"Enough, man! What the fuck is wrong with you? He is her mate, decreed by the Fates! He is her *conpar*. You are nothing to interfere with that," Storm growled, and he shoved Egros hard into the wall, silencing the Witch who seemed stunned by his own hateful words.

"My gods, what have I done? I'm sorry, fuck. Elena, I am sorry. So sorry," Egros groaned, pushing off of Storm and racing from the Keep.

"Oh my gods, Elena? Did Egros really call the Assembly?" Jessenia asked, crouching beside her.

Elena nodded, slumped against the wall, ass on the ground. She was unable to stem the flow of tears. A mix of rage and sorrow falling from her eyes, she glanced over at where Logan remained unmoving.

"Logan," she whispered, but his head was cocked to the side in that way he had when he was deep in thought.

"What is the Assembly?" he asked Storm.

"They're like the Council, but for Guardians. A group of elders and powerful supernaturals who oversee the various groups of Guardians situated throughout the world. They make rulings when there is discord within a group."

"I see. What did he mean her heat cycle?"

"Dude, you gotta ask El. Come on Jess, Storm said gesturing to the other woman to leave them.

Elena listened with dead ears. It was over before it had started. The Assembly was sure to rule against her and Logan. They were certain to order a spell to wipe his memory clean of everything he'd seen and heard. *Of her.*

Dammit. Just the idea of that hurt so damn bad, she could hardly catch her breath. Elena had never been a crier. Not since she'd lost her mom. Even after she'd left her father's house and he refused to see her again. She hadn't cried then. But now? Now her heart was breaking, and the tears would not stop.

Logan remained where he'd stood when he so bravely confronted Egros. He had no idea what the Witch was capable of, but he knew he was a super-natural, and that alone spoke of his boundless bravery.

The distance felt oceans wide, and Elena cringed at the possibilities of what was going through that brilliant mind she'd only begun to skim. She'd gone through packed boxes and boxes with his tools and research. Notebooks that when she'd opened them had blown her mind with the precise details so neatly outlined.

He was indeed methodical and thorough in his

work, as he'd been when he'd made love to her so expertly. Normal or supe, Elena had never had a man so attuned to her every want and need.

Her Panther yowled in despair when she thought of the Assembly and the powers they wielded. The power to take him away before she'd ever really had him.

Head hanging down, she hadn't heard his quiet approach, and she jumped a little when his hands touched her shoulders, then lifted her face to his. Curiosity and surprise shone in his hazel depths as he wiped at her tear stained cheeks.

"Sweetheart, why are you crying?"

"You heard him, Logan. You heard what he said, what he did," she explained.

"All I heard was someone blinded by jealousy rampaging over his own broken heart. He'll get over it. And, if it's important to you, I'll even forgive him for it. But why are *you* so upset?"

"Because you *heard* him," she said, confused. "He told you everything about my heat cycle, and why I was there that night, and you know."

"Elena, let me ask, do all supernaturals go through what you did?"

"No. I mean, I'm a Black Panther and we are kind of loners, but other Cats, Wolves, Mares, and more do experience a heat of some sort. Some males even go into a period of rut," she stated quietly.

She'd never been embarrassed or ashamed of her animal half. The beast was too awesome for that. But she'd always been damn angry when it came to the fact that her heat cycle could possibly dictate the terms of her life. It was grossly unfair.

"I see. So, like your wild cousins, female feline Shifters, and I assume canine Shifters, experience this heat cycle at intense levels. Is that, right?"

She nodded. He was a scientist, surely, he knew what that meant. That for a period of her life she was completely ruled by her hormones, not her own person, at the mercy of her feline's instincts and biological drive to reproduce. Elena cringed, waiting for his judgement

"It's over," he stated.

"What?" She asked, heart stopping at the thought he was leaving forever.

"Your heat. Is it over?" He asked, and she exhaled.

"Yes. After we, um, had sex, my heat receded."

"And normally, when your cycle is present, what do you do?"

"I was taking a potion that is used frequently to

stave off a female's heat cycle. But after a few years it stops being effective."

"I see, biology wins," he said, nodding.

"Logan, I wasn't using you," she tried to explain.

"You were and you weren't. I mean, you needed something, you were acting on instinct, and we clicked. That's fine. Better than," he said and smiled when she wanted to scream. "Elena, it was mind blowing. We were two consenting adults. Human or more than human, and we both wanted each other."

"Yeah," she said, hating the finality in his voice.

"And now?" His warm hazel gaze caught hers, creating fires in her soul, and Elena almost whimpered with desire.

The male was truly so pretty. All angles and hard lines. Contradictions, every last one of them. Even the angry cut of his mouth belied the softness of his lips, the tenderness of his kiss, and the heat she felt in his arms. Her panties dampened, nipples grew hard as her lust for him grew.

"Your friend said something about mates and fate?"

Logan asked, licking his lips and bringing her attention to that oh so talented muscle in his mouth.

"I used to think finding your fated mate was

nothing more than a legend," she whispered in the din of the multi-car garage.

"It's not?"

"No," she replied, shaking her head. "Storm and Fergie, Kingston and Holley, and Furio and Jessenia are three pairs of fated mates who found each other. All live here, in the Keep. We are a family," she said.

"But you don't have one?"

"Well, that's the thing."

"What is?"

"I don't know, Logan. You see, I think maybe I do have a mate."

"How can you be sure it wasn't just your heat?"

His eyes seemed to burn with the question, and Elena's Panther rose within her to meet that golden edged stare of his. Strange and beautiful, never before had she seen such a thing in a human. With wonder she reached for him, kneeling in front of him now on the hard floor, she took his hand and pressed it to the center of her chest.

"Because I feel it here," she replied.

"I think we should try an experiment," he said, licking his lips. "I think we should see if we are compatible without your heat."

"Are you asking me if I'll have sex with you,

Logan?" She grinned, liking his plan very, very much.

"Yeah. I guess I am," her sexy, brilliant normal replied standing before her with one hand extended.

Elena's Panther scratched at her from the inside, urging the woman to accept her mate's hand. But she needed no encouragement from the she-Cat. Elena knew what she wanted, and he was right there.

Mine.

Chapter Thirteen

The blood rushing in Logan's ears made him deaf, dumb, blind to everything but her. Elena pulled him along some dark, secret hallway. Thank fuck she knew where she was going, otherwise he'd never find his way through the Keep again.

"It doesn't matter where you go," Elena explained. "If you don't have a destination in mind, the Keep will take you on a ride through a labyrinth of corridors. It likes to play games."

Interesting, he thought. His scientist's brain could seriously go on overload if he started contemplating magic, and the genetics involved in the passing of magical traits down from one generation to the next. Hell. It thrilled him to know he wasn't crazy after all, and his sample wasn't tainted.

The man from the warehouse was simply not human. And while that explained a little of what he'd found, it opened up a plethora of possibilities and theories. Decades of research, to say the least, and that was just to sate his own personal curiosity.

Still, that sort of pondering was for another time. Elena stopped in front of a door and turned around to face him, pink eyes glowing. Logan's cock went even harder, an impossibility he'd thought for sure.

Well, he'd chalk that up to one of the many things he'd recently had to cross off his *things I know for certain* list. Elena licked her lips, and his mouth watered as he followed the movement of that tiny pink muscle.

"I want you to know, Logan," she said, her naturally husky voice even deeper with need.

The rich tones stroked over him like hands, something a bassist could really appreciate. She wasn't coy or shy, didn't screech and mewl like some simpering idiot. His woman was a warrior goddess, sexy, vibrant, and powerful as fuck. All woman, and all his.

"That when I take you to bed this time, I'm

gonna love you so hard, so long, and so completely, you won't know where you end, and I begin."

"You think I'm easy?" he teased.

"Easy? I don't think there's anything easy about you or this. I'm explaining things to you because I want you to understand, I want you to know, my beautiful man that once we cross this doorway, I plan to lay you bare, strip away all your defenses, and abandon mine. Then I'm gonna give you something I have never offered another living person."

"What's that?" Logan asked, hypnotized by her pale bubble gum stare.

"I'm going to show you what it means to be loved by someone who is dual natured. I'm going to show you my fangs and claws, and I am not going to hold back."

Logan paused a beat, absorbing the impact her words on not just his body, but his mind, and his heart too. He'd always thought believing was seeing, but he was wrong. It was feeling too. And he felt the magic she spoke of pulsating through the hall, flowing from Elena out into the atmosphere and back into him.

Logan was on the brink of the most important discovery of his lifetime, but it wasn't the scientist who benefit most. It was the man. And suddenly, nothing else mattered. Only Elena. Who she was. What she wanted. What she needed. Everything about her. He wanted it all. And in return, he wanted to give her his all.

"I don't want you to hold back. Never with me, sweetheart."

"Good. Because no matter what Egros said about us, I believe you are my fated mate."

"Show me," he growled.

Heart pounding, he waited while she stared, then breathed again as that slow, sexy smile spread across her beautiful face for him. *Only him.* Then it didn't matter if he was only human, and she was a Shifter because she wanted him just as much as he wanted her. And that was a motherfucking miracle.

He tried to be patient. Really, he did as Elena backed him up across the room and shoved him down on the plush comforter of her enormous bed. He had a king, this was nearly double that.

Logan swallowed, taking the shirt off his body while she went for his pants. Impatient little vixen that she was, she tore those fuckers right off, boxers and all. Claw tipped fingers danced across his skin, sending shivers down his body.

Every nerve ending was alight with sensation, and Logan could hardly react. He was drowning in it, in her. That champagne rose bubble gum scent that was all Elena teased him as she settled on her knees between his long legs.

"What are---"

"Shhh," she said, drawing circles on his thighs with her nails as she inched ever so slowly to where he wanted her most.

"Wanna taste you, love. Want you in my mouth."

Elena licked her lips, eyes watching as his cock bobbed on its own. His dick was positively begging for attention as need and desire pulsed through him, beating a tattoo across his brain like a drum. She moaned in pleasure as her lips closed over his mushroomed head, and all rational thought left his brain.

Fuck. Fuck. FUCK.

He'd already suspected he was falling for the woman big time. But if he hadn't known before, this right here was the cincher. She swirled her tongue around the tip, using the rough flat of it to lave the thick vein that ran along the shaft. With one hand around the base, she squeezed, stroked, and sucked him until he thought he was going to go mad with the need to come.

Fuck. And if that wasn't enough, the long silky strands of her silvery platinum hair stroked his thighs like silk. He watched her work him, trying to come to grips with the fact the most beautiful woman he had ever seen in his lifetime was sucking his cock.

She was gorgeous. Brave. Powerful. Sexy. Strong. And she'd picked him of everyone on the planet. He felt honored, humbled, and vowed to prove worthy of her. Fated mates? He might be new to the concept, but he believed her when she said they were meant to be. Knew in his heart she was right about that, because at that moment he also knew he loved her. Irrevocably and completely.

"Elena," he moaned her name, and she purred with her lips around his cock, deep throating him and vibrating the whole time.

He fisted her hair, holding onto the silky silver strands while her head bobbed as she swallowed his dick. The woman was gonna kill him with moves like that.

"Fuck Elena," he moaned. "Elena. Elena. *Elena...*"

Logan panted, repeating her name like a litany. The intensity of the pleasure she was gifting to him. Then the sexy siren squeezed his shaft with one hand and cupped his balls with the other, causing total sensory overload.

Logan came. Hard and fast. Again, she'd rendered him deaf, dumb, and blind to everything but her. When she lifted herself off the floor, releasing his cock with a brilliant popping sound, Logan pulled her on top of him and said the first word that came to mind before flipping their positions.

"Mine."

The singular possessive word came from his mouth, stunning him, and turning her on. They both worked to remove her constrictive clothing, he with his hands and she with her claws.

Fuck. Deadly and handy. Yowza.

Her heart pounded against his, and when he reached between them, his fingers slid easily between the wet folds of her primed sex lips.

Logan dipped his head, sealing his mouth to hers. He wanted to kiss her, needed to like he needed air. Hell, maybe more than. The scientist in him wanted to refute that, but the man shoved the geek deep inside.

He groaned as he sucked on her tongue, still tasting of him while his thumb circled her clit, flicking the tight bud to and fro. He settled his weight on her. Allowing her to feel every inch of him, as he sank into the cradle of her thighs, tasting and touching as much of her as he possibly could.

Was it love that made this sweeter than actual

fucking? Maybe. He couldn't be sure. But damn it, he could kiss Elena Soussa all day and night and never ever grow tired of it. His sweet, sexy kitten growled when he turned his head, kissing her neck and chest.

"Easy kitten, wanna see you, wanna taste you," he said, rubbing circles on her sides, before lifting up to view her pretty, berry tipped breasts.

"Logan," she mewled, back arching as if trying to persuade him to move already.

But he was too busy looking. Heaven was surely missing an angel, because Elena Soussa was there in the bed with him, and she positively glowed like one.

Alabaster skin, silvery hair spread out against the bedspread in a wide circle like wings or a halo even, her pink eyes heavy lidded. She was breathtaking, and he didn't deserve her. But he was too selfish to give her up. Heat or not, he wanted her. And he was gonna work damn hard to ensure she wanted him, too.

He ran his fingers across her chest, lightly skimming her tight nipples and the undersides of each breast. He lifted one to his mouth, swallowed it down, grateful for the moan that tore from her throat.

She was a wildcat then, tugging his head closer as he ran his tongue over her sensitive buds, one then the other. She squirmed beneath him, but he was in no rush. Logan Wells was nothing if not thorough.

"Please," she begged, and he caved. She was much too pretty to beg him.

Logan dipped his hand between them, skimming over her bare mound, dipping into her honeyed heat. Fuck, her pussy was so tight, he groaned as he pressed a second finger inside. Then he was kissing her breasts and finger fucking her in long slow strokes that made his she-Cat wild. Elena panted, gasped, and even growled.

It was hard to believe that a man as alone as Logan was for most of his life could be so wrapped up in a woman he hardly knew. But he was all the same.

Fated mate.

Those words resounded in his head, and the more he thought them, the more they felt right. He never pictured himself married or tied to another human being for his whole life. Maybe this was why. Logan was not meant for another human being. He was meant for *her*.

Elena Soussa was an ass kicking Guardian of Chaos and a Panther Shifter. He was just him. A scientist and amateur musician with a mouthy twin and a pretty decent sized trust fund. But he was not a Shifter, and he had no magic.

Did he deserve her? Maybe not. But he loved her. His heart swelled with each touch and caress, and he knew he could never give her up. She was part of his soul.

Fated mate. This time when he thought it, he pictured his bubble gum eyed kitten smiling at him and he knew they belonged together down to his marrow.

"Please," she begged again, but Logan was not quitting. Not until she purred for him, coming, and saying his name at the same time.

"When I say, kitten," he replied, grinning against the delicious berry that was her nipple.

He could spend the day lavishing attention on her perfect breasts. She huffed out a snarl, but then his thumb moved to swirl around her clit, and his little kitten settled back down. She wanted him to keep going, and he would. Eventually.

Chapter Fourteen

Elena could still taste his spicy male musk on her lips when he kissed her. The fact she knew he could taste himself made her inner kitty yowl and her pussy flood with desire. She wanted him. So. Damn. Badly.

He'd flipped them over and was now working her to rid her of the bothersome clothing she still wore. Why not give him a hand or claw?

"Nice," he murmured and grinned against her lips, tugging the now torn pants off her legs and settling himself in the cradle she made there.

She felt his tight abs against her needy slit and tried pulling him up so she could feel him there, but Logan just grinned some more and shook his head. The bastard.

"Not till I know you're ready, sweetheart," he said, nipping her lip with his blunt teeth, making her nipples pebble against his chest.

"Logan," she moaned his name, feeling petulant that he was making her wait and damn near desperate for him to fill her.

"Patience is a virtue," he whispered, licking her neck and sending spikes of awareness zipping through her tight body.

Mouth wide, she watched as his tongue found her nipples licking slowly around the bud, he kissed and played until he finally sucked the whole thing into his mouth, making her cry out loud into the darkness. He paid the same attention to her other breast, kissing and licking her creamy white flesh until she almost couldn't stand it.

Then, same as before, he sucked her nipple inside the hot cavern of his mouth, pulling and tugging with his mouth, causing the most amazing sensations to spark through her flesh. The man was torturously thorough.

Going back for more, he paid close attention to every inch of her breasts. Every speck and morsel, every crevice and freckle, until he'd tasted each tiny little bit of flesh. Logan moaned and whispered sweet words to her, kissing her the whole time. Like he was stamping himself all over her ever so slowly. Maybe he was simply out to drive her crazy while he did.

Who was she kidding? Elena fucking loved it.

Sliding further down her sizzling skin, Logan slid, kissing, and licking along the way. He pressed her knees apart, opening her up nice and wide for him.

"Look at you so pretty and pink, sweetheart. Delicious," he growled much like a beast though she knew he was not.

Then he was kissing her there, and Elene was unconcerned with their differences. Her only thought was he better not stop. Not until she came, for fuck's sake. Elena leaned back, holding onto the headboard as he swirled his tongue around her clit.

So good. He was so damn good. His long body moved as he ate her, the muscles in his back rippling with each ministration. Fuck, he really was beautiful. And he was hers.

Her she-Cat roared with a possessiveness she'd never felt, and it flowed through her making everything all the more intense. She never wanted him to go, needed him in her life, couldn't wait to tell him.

Then his fingers joined his mouth, two thick ones pressing deep inside her while he doubled his efforts with his tongue lapping at her clit. Elena almost came then, but he slowed down, teasing her so good.

"Oh gods," she moaned, fisting his hair, and pushing him harder against her sex.

Elena opened her legs wider, bucking against him. She loved how he was with her, aggressive and demanding, but tender, so fucking tender even as he set the pace. She loved his reaction to her every response. When he moaned and growled against her clit, pumping his fingers harder and faster, she saw stars.

When she finally came, she screamed his name. Pulling him by his hair, he lifted his head.

"Condoms?"

"Don't need them. I don't contract STDs, and I am only fertile during my heat."

"Really?"

"Uh huh," she nodded, grabbing his cock and lining it up right where she needed him.

"Watch, sweetheart. Watch us become one," Logan commanded, lifting up so that the tip of his magnificent dick was just kissing her pussy, then, ever so slowly, he pressed inside.

Awareness, anticipation, and pure, unadulterated joy filled her as she did what he said and watched. It was the single most erotic thing that had ever happened to Elena. They groaned in unison when he filled her to the hilt. Sighing initially with relief, Elena found herself whimpering as wave after wave of desire swept through her.

"Logan," she said his name, practically begging him to move.

But her sweet, sexy normal would not be rushed. He nuzzled her neck, teeth grazing her skin, hands roaming her arms and chest, her face, her belly, breasts, and hips. On and on, his talented fingers roamed, grazing, touching, learning every inch of her. And still he did not move.

Elena growled, but he had her wrists, pinning them with one hand. Sure, she could break free, but why would she want to? She tried flexing her hips, turned her head to capture his mouth in a kiss, but he evaded her, dropping small, whisper light touches along her jaw and neck, breastbone, and nipples.

"Do you know how beautiful you are, sweetheart? I was captivated by you from the very first second in that club. Hell, I think I felt you come into the room before I ever saw you."

His words caressed her, warmed her deep inside, but it was the long, slow flex and withdraw of his enormous cock that drew a long, guttural moan from her lips.

In and out, roll, flex, withdraw. Logan fucked her ever so slowly. Talking all the while, giving her just enough to keep her from begging, and yet, he kept her wanting more. Always more. She was starving for him and drowning in him at the same time.

"So sweet, love, like bubble gum and champagne roses. Want you to purr for me," he whispered, tugging her nipple with his teeth while he increased his pace just a tad.

His big hands ran down her back, under her ass, lifting her, tilting her hips, and deeper he went. His cock felt so good, stretching her, stroking her in just that right spot. Elena's Panther pushed forward, elongating her fangs, and unleashing her claws. She growled and panted, swirling her hips every time he plunged into her wet heat. Looking for release, chasing that elusive sliver of euphoria that was just out of reach.

"Gonna get you there, baby. No rush."

"Please," she whimpered.

"When I say, kitten," he smirked, and she could've socked him, but just then he changed the angle and Elena's eyes crossed.

Fucking hell.

She'd never felt like this. Weak and at the mercy of a man's touch. She was open, vulnerable, needy for him. That alone was new. The fact she wasn't angry or frightened by the sudden shift of power told her she was correct. Her Panther knew it all along. Logan Wells was hers.

"Trust me?" Logan asked, hazel eyes blazing with passion in the dark bedroom.

"Always," she replied without hesitation.

"Hold on, baby," he growled, biting her lower lip, reaching down to lift her knees over his wrists.

Logan spread her wide, grinding into her, he pressed and pressed, swirling his hips in an erotic dance that had him hitting her spot just right. Elena's whole body vibrated then, a deep, seductive tremble that racked her from head to toe.

Starting where his cock fed her pussy, lightning bolts of pleasure began to strike out to engulf her entire body. Claws scratched at his shoulders, marking him as hers, but she couldn't stop herself, couldn't control it. Nothing like this had ever happened to her.

She'd never lost control like this, but this time, Elena let herself go. She gave the power to Logan and moaned in unrivaled pleasure as he took the reins readily. Her orgasm rolled through her, slowly and completely. So fucking hard, she almost blacked out from the strength of it.

Elena could hardly do more than ride the wave of bliss as it crashed into her. Curling her toes, arching her back, she screamed his name, then rearing up, she did the unthinkable. Elena gave him her mating bite, closed her fangs over his neck and bit down binding herself to him for life, without asking, without explaining, she'd marked Logan Wells.

"Mine!" She roared and felt him stiffen as his own orgasm exploded through him, filling her so completely.

Logan came and came, and she reveled in the explosive passion that erupted between them. After he collapsed on top of her, thoroughly spent and sated, she licked the place she bit him, closing the wound and kissing the skin there.

"That was," he panted, trying to catch his breath.

"Mmm," she whispered, kissing his shoulder and his cheek.

"I mean, I never. Even the first time, it was never like this." He grinned, kissing her hard, then slowly easing out of her.

Already she missed him there. Wanted his cock buried deep in her body. Always.

"Elena, talk to me. You look so worried. What is it?"

Shit.

She really had to explain. Needed to tell him exactly what this all meant. It had never been her life's plan to find a mate and leave the Guardians, but with the Assembly already on their way, what other choice did she have?

"I marked you," she began.

"The bite?" His eyes narrowed as he listened.

"Shifters, other supes, sometimes bite during sex. But the bite I just gave you was a mating bite. Shifters give that bite only to their mates."

"So, I'm your mate. You know now it wasn't your heat," he grinned, and her heart pounded in response.

Dammit. He was so beautiful. And he didn't seem angry in the least.

"I should have asked you first. I am so sorry. I just got, well, carried away." Elena winced at how idiotic she seemed.

"Hey, look at me," Logan traced her cheek, then with a firm forefinger on her chin tilted her face toward his.

"I love you, Elena. I want to be yours, so if that means you biting me and giving me the most intense orgasm I have ever known, I am so down, baby."

"Yeah?"

"Oh, yeah. In fact," he cupped her face in his hands and kissed her again, his renewed passion jutting against her hip, and Elena moaned in pleasure.

Her future might not be in stone, but this was. Logan belonged to her now, and she to him. Whatever else happened, that was a truth no one could deny.

Many hours later, wrapped around each other, someone knocked on her bedroom door.

"El?" Fergie's voice called to them, and Logan sat up, but Elena stilled him with a hand on his arm.

"El? The Assembly representative is here. Kingston said you should come to the conference room."

Her heart pounded in her chest as she thought of the implications. There was no way she was going to let them take Logan and bespell him. Panic filled her, making her tremble, then he was there, in front of her.

"Hey, look at me. Whatever happens, I am with you, Elena. Me and you, together. Got it?"

"Okay."

Chapter Fifteen

"Elena, Logan," Kingston opened the door to the conference room and stepped back to allow them both to enter.

The Dragon's face was a mask, and she felt her nerves tense. Storm, Furio, Byram, and Egros were there as well. Each male looked at her and nodded, except the male Witch. His shamed eyes did not meet hers.

Traitor, she thought angrily, but Logan's fingers gripped hers and she knew forgiveness was not far away. Egros was misguided, but he was not evil. Still, she was not quite ready to make that leap. Not when her whole life was about to change forever.

Sitting at the long conference table was a

stranger. The Assembly representative, she concluded. The man was dressed in a long robe with a mask over his face, hiding his identity. She looked at Kingston curiously, but he was impassive.

"You are Elena Soussa?"

"Yes," she answered the stranger.

"This is your *human*," the Assembly rep spat the word as if it were dirty, angering Elena.

"My name is Logan Wells. You are?"

"You dare address me? Silence. This does not concern you," snarled the man.

"Sir, I think if you take a moment to listen you might be pleasantly surprised. You see, I'm a scientist, a geneticist and biochemist to be precise. I believe I can help the Guardians in this fight to keep magic free."

"How could you possibly hope to help?"

"For one thing, I spent a few minutes analyzing the Gila Shifter saliva, and after talking with Holley, I believe I can help make a preventive elixir to ward off the paralytic effects of their venom."

"That is insane. No Witch has ever been able---"

"That's because each potion will need to be created for each individual. Time consuming, but worth it, sir."

"Don't interrupt again, normal. My concern is for the Guardians as a whole, and you are not even supposed to know about us, *normal,*---"

"That's it. You will stop calling him that, right now. His name is Logan."

Elena's pink eyes flashed angrily and before everyone gathered pink flames began to lick her skin coming out of nowhere at all. Her eyes blazed, the reflection in the glass hutch behind the representative, and she watched in awe as pink flames billowed from her ears and from between her parted lips.

"You! You are fate marked!" yelled the shocked Representative.

"I am," she replied. "He is my fated mate, and I am a Guardian of Chaos, sir. The Keep is our home, and I shall do my duty with my *conpar* by my side."

"And you, Kingston Baldric? You are the leader of this group. What say you?"

Elena blinked as her flames receded, noting Logan had held firm to her hand the entire time. The flames had not hurt him. Joy pulsed through her as she realized that, if anything, he seemed to think she was really cool.

"Love you," he murmured, and she felt herself blush all the way down to her panties.

Storm cleared his throat, and Elena's eyes flashed to their Alpha, who waited for her attention before turning to the Assembly representative. This was going to be tricky, and she tensed waiting for her leader's response.

"Our group is more than just the average Guardians, sir. My team is a Pack, a family. So before I answer, I will ask their answers," then Kingston turned to the other Guardians, some of whom had suddenly been joined by their mates. "What say you of Elena's mate?"

The hush in the room grew exponentially as each Guardian eyed one another. Elena held in her next breath. Her entire future was now in the hands of those she'd called family for so long.

As with all families, they'd had their difficulties over the years and decades they'd lived and worked together. But this was the first time she was unsure of the outcome. She supposed it was because nothing had ever mattered so much to her.

Logan squeezed her hand, and she silently thanked the gods for him. He was the only man who had ever been there solely for her support and comfort. It meant so much to her. She hoped to pay him back in kind, or to at least be afforded the opportunity.

One thing became quite apparent to her in that long stretch of silence. If the strange Assembly Representative ruled against her, against Logan, she would walk away from her vow and from the Guardians forever.

And the second she owned that, peace settled over her. Logan stood, brows furrowed, but she caught his gaze. He watched her silently, then a small smile teased the corner of his mouth, and some- how, through their *matebond* perhaps, Elena knew he understood her. Even better, she knew in her very bones that he felt the same. No matter what, they would be together, and that was enough for both of them.

"Doc's cool," Storm replied, blue eyes flashing at Fergie. He was the first to break the silence, and Elena's pulse raced with joy.

"I agree. He's awesome. Even likes my shoes," Fergie answered with a playful wink at Logan, earning her a stern growl from her mate.

"Oh hush," she told her besotted Wolf. "You know you're the only one for me."

"I better be."

"We think Doc is the man, too," Furio stepped forward, rolling his eyes at the Wolf pair. He had his hand on the small of Jessenia's back, and the kitchen Witch nodded in agreement.

"He's already helped me with his knowledge of genetics to improve my herb garden. I expect our elixirs and potions to be exponentially stronger this coming year," she added helpfully.

"Apologies, I have not yet made Logan's acquaintance," Byram, the only Vampire among them spoke up. "However, if Elena vouches for him, then I see no problem. She has proved herself a hardworking and dedicated Guardian time and again. I trust her implicitly," Byram bowed slightly, and Elena nodded.

The Vampire was perhaps the most secretive of them all, but that was simply his nature. He was powerful, strong, and he'd never treated her as anything other than equal. She respected him. The fact he trusted her and said so aloud made her very happy to call him friend.

"I think Dr. Wells is just brilliant," Holley offered. "And if our Elena says he is her mate, then that is what he is, and I see no issues for their future. Neither do the *manetuwak* who've already acclimated to Logan's preferences." The Witch spoke with a twinkle in her eye.

The moment Holley mentioned the spirits of the

Keep, the lights fluttered, changing from a gold color to the soft white glow that Elena knew Logan liked better. The Representative gasped, head turning to Kingston, but the Dragon smiled lovingly at his mate. Elena felt Logan's hands tense around hers as Egros stepped forward.

"Sir, I am the one who called you here," the male Witch. "My name is Egros Pyke. I who called the Assembly to investigate the normal Logan Wells and his relationship with Elena Soussa, my fellow Guardian. I want to offer my sincere apologies to them both. You see," Egros said, clearing his throat and glancing at Elena and Logan before quickly turning his remorseful eyes to the Representative. "I was overcome with jealousy. She'd refused my offer to help see her through her heat cycle, and I was wounded. I see now that my affection was misplaced and ill advised. Elena Soussa was never anything but loyal and professional. A true Guardian that I would do well to model myself after."

"I see Mr. Pyke," the Representative replied. "And what say you, now of Logan Wells?"

"I say Dr. Wells is the true fated mate, the *conpar* of Elena Soussa, Guardian of Chaos, Panther Shifter, and my friend, if she will forgive me. I am hoping they both will, actually." He grimaced then reached behind him and held out his offering.

"Uh, I know it's not much, but I retrieved this for you," he said, holding Logan's bass out to her mate.

"Thank you," Logan said, and he moved forward to retrieve his *Rickenbacker Fireglo*, highly polished and looking good as new, from the Witch.

Stepping back, Logan's arm came around Elena's waist and he nodded encouragingly. She inhaled his spicy scent, calming her Panther, and relieving some of her anger. She was still upset, but she knew she could not stay angry with Egros and remain there. And she very much wanted to do just that, with Logan by her side.

"I see. So that leaves me then," the masked Representative faced Elena and Logan. Tension had her straightening her back, she felt her newly mate given powers circling them both and looked down to see pink flames dancing at her fingertips.

"I have one question for the couple," he said in a voice that suddenly seemed quite familiar to Elena.

Like something lost from a memory she had pushed to the foremost corner of her mind. Elena stepped closer to the tall stranger. Tears unexpectedly pricked her eyes, as he reached behind him and removed his mask.

"And that is, can you forgive an old fool?"

"Papa?" Elena cried out, throwing herself at the man who'd forced her to choose a life without him when she took her vows.

"Elena, mija, can you ever forgive me? I was so lost in my fears and my grief, I forgot what was important, my daughter. I've spent years trying to gather the courage to approach you."

"But the Assembly? How?"

"I have contacts," her father shrugged, and wiped his face unashamedly.

"Hello, sir. I'm Logan," her mate stepped forward offering his hand, but Anthony Soussa grabbed him in a hug and kissed both his cheeks.

"Thank you, son. You be good to my Elena, now."

"Of course," he replied, smiling as she tucked herself into his side, sighing happily while the rest of their group erupted in conversation and laughter.

Champagne was opened, and glasses shared as they toasted the end of the inquiry and a new chapter for one of their own. After a few hours of catching up, Elena's father left with a promise to visit for Easter.

That night as she lay wrapped around her mate, Elena sighed and snuggled into his warm skin. Logan grunted and opened his sleepy eyes to gaze at her with such love and emotion, she could hardly dare to believe it was real.

"It's real, kitten. I love you so much. More than my life," he whispered, kissing her temple.

"I love you too. I'm so happy, I feel like I could burst. Are you going to be happy here though? I mean, I am asking you to give up your life---"

"What life? Elena, I work for myself and the lab the Keep has already started putting together for me is better than anything I ever had at home or in any office. I am going to be working with Byram, Holley, and Egros on new potions that will help all of you, protect you, my love, and I couldn't be happier. As a matter of fact, look," he leaned over and picked up a vial, handing it to her.

"What is it?"

"It's a new potion to stop a female Shifter's heat. I ran an analysis of the one you used to take that stopped working and discovered why the potion was losing its effectiveness. We just needed to apply the principals of precision medicine, personalizing each dose to the different Shifter species," Logan said, sitting up as his excitement grew.

He was so brilliant and gifted. Elena sat up with him, lost in his energetic speech. To say she was surprised was a gross understatement. This meant so much to her and would mean as much to so many other females. Having to go through a heat cycle robbed many of their choices, but this would offer to put the control back in their hands.

"The one size fits all method was not working efficiently because you are all so genetically diverse. We had your sample on file, so I was able to tailor this to you."

"What about when I want to," she said, blushing furiously.

"Have children?" He asked with a wide, warm grin.

"You simply stop taking the potion. From what I can see, your Shifter genes are hardwired to heal and protect you. The second you decide you want to have kids, sweetheart, all you do is let your heat cycle start and let nature take its course."

"And you're okay, waiting?"

"To start a family? Yes, I am more than okay doing whatever you want, my love. I want children with you, but there is no rush. Being with you has made me the happiest man in the world. I would do anything for you," he said, cupping her cheek and kissing her softly.

"Do you mean that?"

"Of course."

"Then make love to me, Logan. Show me how you feel about me."

And he did. Again and again, until she came purring his name.

Prrr. Logan. Mine. Mate.

Epilogue

Holley grimaced and rubbed her belly as she, Jessenia, and Fergie waited for Elena to step out of the cubby where she was trying on her wedding gown. The *Ladies' Room* had the *Rat Pack* softly playing in the background and snow was falling outside the large windows that faced the woods.

It was a chilly March morning, but the friends were more than happy to gather around the cozy fireplace to plan Logan and Elena's upcoming nuptials. He'd proposed almost immediately after moving into the Keep, and she'd said yes.

"Come on, El. I'm starving," Fergie bellowed despite the bowl of buttery popcorn on her lap.

"You're always hungry," Jessenia teased.

"*Shyaddap*," Fergie snorted, throwing a kernel at her bestie.

"Will you two, quit it," Holley grumbled, hand on her back.

"Are you, okay?" Jessenia asked.

"Yeah, yeah. I'm fine. My little one is just messing my back up," Holley tried to laugh as she grasped her back with one hand and clutched her enormous belly with the other.

"El? You might want to speed this up," Jessenia called out, her eyes still riveted to the heavily pregnant Witch.

"She's nervous, isn't that cute? Hey, El, can I ask you something?"

"What is it, Ferg?"

"Well, since you're now a one man gal, does that make you *pussy whipped*?"

"*What?*"

"*What?*"

"*What?!*"

All three women replied but Fergie was on a roll, munching popcorn and talking to no one in particular, she continued.

"Yeah, I totally think *pussy whipped* applies to you. I mean A) you have a pussy, and B) you turn into a pussy, and C) the aforementioned pussy is being fucked by one guy which essentially makes you---"

"Uh, Fergie, no," Jessenia said. "That is so not how you use that phrase!"

"What? I think I'm totally right," the redhead said but before she could really get into it, Elena roared, grabbing everyone's attention.

"Thank you! Alright, I am coming out now. No one laugh," Elena called, and stepped out onto the runway.

All three women stopped and stared. There was no laughter at all, not even a smile. Elena bit her lip and tried not to fidget.

"Well?" she asked, nervously looking down at the vintage, off the shoulder, mermaid gown.

It was made entirely of Leavers lace and silk, the color a blush tinted ivory that made her eyes glow. Of the five gowns the Keep had offered, one look, and she'd fallen in love with it.

"Oh El!" Jessenia sighed, clutching her hands to her chest.

"You are so beautiful!" Fergie said.

"Holley?" Elena's eyes went to Holley, who was tearing up as she gazed at her friend.

"It's perfect, El. Take it off."

"What?"

"Take it off, now," Holley growled.

"Why?" Elena asked.

"Holley!" Fergie barked.

"Because I'm in labor! Ooooh!" The Witch bellowed.

Everyone moved like lightning. Jessenia called Furio who went to get Kingston from the green-house. Fergie put her arm around Holley to help her stand, while Elena stepped out of the wedding dress, shrugging into her tank top and jeans before going to pick Holley up and off the ground.

She'd barely stepped into the hallway with her when Kingston came flying down the hallway. He took his mate and headed to the infirmary.

"Byram is waiting in the medical wing, love. Just hold on. Elena, call Logan and Egros!"

"On it," she yelled back.

Logan and Egros had developed a tentative friendship that had allowed both males to work together to create potions, elixirs, and medicines that would help supernaturals the world over. One of them was designed to lessen the risk of complications during labor since birthrates were dangerously low for some supes.

We're on our way.

She reread Logan's text and immediately

calmed. Her mate was coming, and he would do all he could to help her friend. Apparently, when he'd told them about his doctorates, Logan had failed to mention graduating from med school.

"I never got my license to practice."

He'd said and shrugged it off. This was after she'd confronted him when her mate had helped set a bone in Furio's leg when he'd unexpectedly broke it after engaging with some Loyalists during a mission. Logan was full of surprises, and so far, she loved every one of them.

Hours later...

The sounds of a baby's cries echoed through the halls as Storm, Furio, Elena, and their mates gathered in the kitchen for some snacks. Soon, Egros and Byram shuffled in after them.

It had been an exhausting process for everyone, but none more than Holley and her dragonling. The baby, named Greyson Mount Baldric, was resting now with his doting parents.

"How are they?" Elena asked Egros, and he smiled and nodded.

"Mother and babe are very well. Kingston looks like he needs a stiff drink though," he said with a snort of laughter echoed by the others.

Happiness seemed to overflow the Keep as

Jessenia prepared some grilled cheese sandwiches and homemade tomato soup. Furio helped his mate by dishing up the food and serving everyone. It was delicious, and they ate and joked around as a feeling of complete serenity washed over them.

Snow continued to fall, and Elena sat on Logan's lap, feeding him bites of grilled cheese and kissing him every chance she got. She looked at the pink sapphire on her finger and smiled.

He'd worked with Egros to bespell the band to stretch when she shifted to her Panther, and to shrink again when she switched back. So thoughtful, she sighed kissing his soft lips once more.

"Are you sure you want to wear it all the time?"

"I'm sure. It's a sign of our commitment to each other. I'll never take it off," she murmured, pleased when she saw his happiness in the radiance of his smile.

So lost in their glow of love, neither Logan nor Elena noticed the woman drop from the sky right outside the window. That was not until she busted right through it pointing two military grade weapons, one at Elena's face and the other at Egros' balls. The male Witch snarled angrily, having jumped up to defend the couple as soon as he realized what was happening.

"Get the fuck off my brother!" snarled the female.

"Margo! Margo, what the hell are you doing?"

Why did Elena recognize that name? Shit. His sister. That was his sister, Elena thought curiously. The short woman had gold brown skin and a head full of glossy black curls. The only similarity between them was her large hazel eyes.

"Rescuing you from these people. You don't know what they are, Logan---"

Elena jumped off him and stood in a defensive position. No way in hell was anyone taking her mate. She felt her Panther's anger, looked down to see pink flames swirling around her fingers.

"Oh shit. I've never seen a Shifter do that!"

"How the hell do you know about Shifters?" Logan asked her.

"How do *you* know about them?" She asked back.

Brother and sister bickered while the rest of the Guardians and their mates shrugged and went back to their food. The window repaired itself, and only Egros and Elena remained with Margo and Logan.

The male Witch seemed paralyzed, maybe because of the gun still pointed at him, or maybe because the violent little woman was truly something to behold. Elena grinned, then stepped beside her mate.

"My name is Elena, and Logan and I are mated."

"Mated? OMG! She brainwashed you," Margo said through gritted teeth.

"What? No, I did not!"

"We're engaged, Margo," he said proudly.

"Engaged?"

"Yes, and I think you better sit down and tell us what the hell is going on," Logan said eyes narrowed at his now squirming sister.

"How did you find us?" Egros asked, reminding everyone of his presence.

"Okay, fine. I will tell you everything, but do you have anymore of that soup? It was cold as hell out there."

Elena laughed and took her new sister-in-law by the hand. She and Logan led her to the dining room table, Elena fully aware of Egros' eyes on the small human. Once she had her settled with a bowl, deep in discussion with Fergie about the latest Ferragamo boots, she called Logan over.

"Well? How do you think she knew about us?"

"Margo has been involved with secret government ops for years. Your guess is as good as mine," he shrugged.

"I have another question," Elena said, loving how he took her waist and pulled her flush against him.

"What's that, kitten?"

"Will she be okay on her own for a few while you and I sneak back to our room?"

Logan glanced at his sister, then back at his mate. His grin wicked as he took her hand and headed down the hall, calling out to Fergie to find Margo a room for the night and telling his sis that he'd see her in the morning.

"But Logan---" Margo yelled after him.

"Tomorrow," he called back.

Lifting Elena in his arms, he took off at a run to their room. She giggled and held on, not used to that sort of thing. But her human mate was full of surprises, and she looked forward to more with each passing day.

"Now, what did you have in mind, kitten?"

"Let me show you," she said, mashing her mouth to his.

Her inner kitty purred deeply as their matebond pulsed and swirled around them. Logan and Elena's love, so precious and new, was strong and pure, and full of loyalty and integrity. She kissed him with every one of those things in her heart, pouring all her love and desire into it. Making sure he knew just what he meant to her with every slide and swipe of her tongue against his.

"I love you, Elena."

"I love you too, Logan. I would die for you."

"Don't do that, mate. Live for me instead. My own *Panther Incensed*. And I promise to live for you, every single day."

T he end.

Did you like the story? Read the rest of the Guardians of Chaos today!

P.S

Don't forget to tell me how you liked this story by leaving your honest review! *No pressure.* 😉

A review can be one or two brief sentences where you simply state whether you enjoyed the story and would recommend it to someone! It is an enormous help to authors and the best way for us to reach larger audiences so we can keep writing the stories you love!

Thank you so much!

Xoxo!

Del mare alla stella,

C.D. Gorri

Have you met my Dragons?

The Falk Clan Tales are my stories surrounding four Dragon Shifter brothers and how they find their one true mates.

Each brother's chest is marked with his rose, the magical link to his heart and his magic. They each have a matching gemstone to go with it.

She's given up on love, but he's just begun.

In *The Dragon's Valentine* we meet the eldest Falk brother, Callius. He is on a mission to find a Castle and his one true mate, one he can trust with his diamond rose....

His heart is frozen; can she change his mind about love?

In *The Dragon's Christmas Gift* our attention shifts to Alexsander, the youngest brother of the four. He has resigned himself to a life alone, until he meets *her*.

Some wounds run deep, can a Dragon's heart be unbroken?

The Dragon's Heart is the story of Edric Falk who has vowed never to love again, but that changes when he meets his feisty mate, Joselyn Curacao.

She just wants a little fun, he's looking for a lifetime.

We finally meet Nikolai Falk and his sexy Shifter mate in *The Dragon's Secret*.

**Now available in a boxed set.*

Look for The Dragon's Treasure in 2022!

Connect with C.D. Gorri

To learn more about me please visit:

https://www.cdgorri.com

https://www.facebook.com/Cdgorribooks

https://twitter.com/cgor22

https://www.bookbub.com/authors/c-d-gorri

TikTok

Visit my website to find out more about my supernatural world also known as the Grazi Kelly Universe and sign up to be a subscriber!

https://www.cdgorri.com/newsletter

Have you met my Bears?

Looking for a Paranormal Romance series that is loads of growly fun?

Meet the Barvale Clan first in the Bear Claw Tales! A complete shifter romance series about 4 brothers who discover and need to win their fated mates!

Followed by two more spin off series, the Barvale Clan Tales and the Barvale Holiday Tales!

No cliffhangers. Steamy PNR fun. Go and read your next happily ever after today!

Other Titles by C.D. Gorri

Other Titles by C.D. Gorri

Young Adult Urban Fantasy Books:

Wolf Moon: A Grazi Kelly Novel Book 1

Hunter Moon: A Grazi Kelly Novel Book 2

Rebel Moon: A Grazi Kelly Novel Book 3

Winter Moon: A Grazi Kelly Novel Book 4

Chasing The Moon: A Grazi Kelly Short 5

Blood Moon: A Grazi Kelly Novel 6

*Get all 6 books NOW AVAILABLE IN A BOXED SET:

The Complete Grazi Kelly Novel Series

Casting Magic: The Angela Tanner Files 1

Keeping Magic: The Angela Tanner Files 2

G'Witches Magical Mysteries Series

Co-written with P. Mattern

G'Witches

G'Witches 2: The Hary Harbinger

Home for the Howlidays: A Macconwood Pack Tale 6

A Silver Wedding: A Macconwood Pack Tale 7

Mine Furever: A Macconwood Pack Tale 8

A Furry Little Christmas: A Macconwood Pack Tale 9

Also available in two boxed sets:

The Macconwood Pack Tales Volume 1

Shifters Furever: The Macconwood Pack Tales Volume 2

The Falk Clan Tales:

The Dragon's Valentine: A Falk Clan Novel 1

The Dragon's Christmas Gift: A Falk Clan Novel 2

The Dragon's Heart: A Falk Clan Novel 3

The Dragon's Secret: A Falk Clan Novel 4

The Dragon's Treasure: A Falk Clan Novel 5

Dragon Mates: The Falk Clan Complete Series Boxed Set Books 1-4

The Bear Claw Tales:

Bearly Breathing: A Bear Claw Tale 1

Bearly There: A Bear Claw Tale 2

Bearly Tamed: A Bear Claw Tale 3

Bearly Mated: A Bear Claw Tale 4

Also available in a boxed set:

The Complete Bear Claw Tales (Books 1-4)

Bound by Air: The Wardens of Terra Book 1

Star Kissed: A Wardens of Terra Short

Waterlocked: The Wardens of Terra Book 2

Moon Kissed: A Wardens of Terra Short

*Now in a boxed set and in audio!

The Maverick Pride Tales:

Purrfectly Mated: Paranormal Dating Agency: A Maverick Pride Tale 1

Purrfectly Kissed: Paranormal Dating Agency: A Maverick Pride Tale 2

Purrfectly Trapped: Paranormal Dating Agency: A Maverick Pride Tale 3

Purrfectly Caught: Paranormal Dating Agency: A Maverick Pride Tale 4

Purrfectly Naughty: Paranormal Dating Agency: A Maverick Pride Tale 5

Purrfectly Bound: Paranormal Dating Agency: A Maverick Pride Tale 6

Also available in 2 boxed sets:

The Maverick Pride Volume 1

The Maverick Pride Volume 2

Dire Wolf Mates:

Shake That Sass: Sassy Ever After: Dire Wolf Mates Book 1

Breaking Sass: Sassy Ever After: Dire Wolf Mates 2

Pinch of Sass: Sassy Ever After: Dire Wolf Mates 3

Also available in a boxed set:

Dire Wolf Mates Volume 1

Wyvern Protection Unit:

Trusting Her Protector

Tempting Her Protector

Tricking Her Protector

Standalones:

The Enforcer

Blood Song: A Sanguinem Council Book

EveL Worlds:

Chinchilla and the Devil: A FUCN'A BookSammi and the Jersey Bull: A FUCN'A Book

The Guardians of Chaos:

Wolf Shield: Guardians of Chaos Book 1

Dragon Shield: Guardians of Chaos Book 2

Stallion Shield: Guardians of Chaos Book 3

Panther Shield: Guardians of Chaos 4

Howl's Romance

Mated to the Werewolf Next Door: A Howl's Romance

The Tiger King's Christmas Bride

Claiming His Virgin Mate: Howls Romance

Twice Mated Tales

Doubly Claimed

Doubly Bound

Doubly Tied

Hearts of Stone Series

Shifter Mountain: Hearts of Stone 1

Shifter City: Hearts of Stone 2

Accidentally Undead Series

Fangs For Nothin'

Moongate Island Tales

Moongate Island Mate

Mated in Hope Falls

Mated by Moonlight

Shifters Unleashed Boxed Sets

*Check out these amazing anthologies where you can find
some of my books*

and the works of other awesome authors!

Coming Soon:

Ash: Speed Dating with the Denizens of Hell

Hungry Like Her Wolf: Magic and Mayhem Universe

Shifter Village: Hearts of Stone 3

Excerpt from Code Wolf

"Are you fuckin' with me?"

"No, Randall, I assure you I am not fuckin' with you," Rafe Maccon eased his immense frame back into his oversized, black leather chair and narrowed his ice blue eyes at his Third and one of his oldest friends. How long had he known the man sitting in front of him?

Randall had come to Maccon City when Rafe was about ten, he looked the same then as he did now. Tall at six foot three inches, muscular, and more than a little intimidating to the Wolves under him with his long beard and equally long dark brown hair.

Rafe, however, was the Alpha. He was more amused than intimidated by his surly friend.

"A vacation?! What the fuck am I gonna do on a vacation? Come on, Rafe, this is bullshit!"

The door to Rafe's private office flew open and in strolled a very happy, very pregnant Charley Maccon, Rafe's wife. The Alpha's eyes glowed as they landed on his positively glowing mate. She wore a long, flowy dress. The shade was a pale-yellow color that, Randall admitted to himself, looked damn good with her creamy complexion and curly dark hair.

Their Alpha Female was quite something. There wasn't a Wolf Guard in the place who wouldn't lay down his/her life for her.

"Well, maybe you should consider a vacation to be a relaxing experience, Randy," she dropped a kiss on Randall's cheek and walked past him, over to her husband whom she kissed full on the mouth.

The way his Alpha's eyes homed in on her when she opened the door was nothing compared to the hungry gaze that followed her across the room.

Randall had noticed it took a while for Rafe to get used to his mate's habit of greeting everyone with a kiss or hug. Wolves were protective of their mates, but Randall thought his Alpha was doing an exceedingly good job of hiding his tension. Werewolves did not share very well.

Charley; however, had stood firm. That was the way she was raised, and she wasn't going to change for any, how had she put it? Neanderthal browbeating husband, regardless of how cute his ass was!

Randall had no direct knowledge if the "cute ass" statement was true or not. And he didn't want to know. He liked Charley though, had from the beginning. He was musically inclined and often took to one of the common rooms to strum his guitar or play a few keys on the piano.

Excerpt from Shifter Mountain
by C.D. Gorri

Keeton's Mountain Lion hissed angrily as he boarded the plane for the States. Three months on Moongate Island did nothing to repair his faith in people. Shifter or human, they pretty much sucked.

True, he was no longer being blackmailed by the sniveling cretin who'd been part of his last black ops assignment. Fucker had stepped on a landmine deep in the jungles of a place Keeton was not at liberty to name. Not even in his own head.

Fucking hell.

Yeah, it meant he could return home now, but to who? Keeton had no family waiting for him. His few friends were back on the island, but that was no place for his inner feline. The beast craved the hills and valleys of the New Jersey forests he called home.

He'd bought a hundred acres of forest off the beaten paths of New Jersey's Panther Mountains years ago. Even commissioned the building of a cabin deep in the woods. The design was environmentally conscientious and entirely sound. Two stories high, it had its own generators, additional solar paneling, and wind turbines for power, and indoor plumbing.

He wasn't an animal, for fuck's sake. But even if Keeton was going to avoid people, he didn't have to be uncomfortable doing it. Eyes closed, he sat seemingly at ease, but he was keeping tabs on every living thing around him on the plane.

Once a soldier, always a soldier, his two commanders, Callan McGregor and Landry Smyth, had said that often enough. Both men were Shifters, a unique Alpha and Omega pair who'd completed their Triad once they'd found their mate in Sage Freeman, a smart mouthed human female. That had been Keeton's cue to leave the island he'd called home for eighty-nine and a half days.

They hadn't kicked him out or anything. On the contrary. But he was restless and antsy. The island could no longer contain his need for isolation.

Memories of the disgust on Bruce Taylor's face when he'd seen Keeton lose control of his shift during a particularly bloody battle were forever ingrained in his brain. The human male had been a new recruit in the special ops task force where Keeton had served his country for the last five years in secret.

Dismantling dictatorships and stopping atrocities the likes of which he could hardly put a name to before they could ever see the light of day had been his job, and blackmail was his reward.

He'd kept the fact that he'd unwittingly told the secret about Shifters to the human from Callan and Landry until the night Bruce had died believing Keeton was the only one of his kind. The two men had investigated his claims, making sure that he never downloaded or emailed the proof he'd recorded with his phone the night Keeton lost control.

The half a million dollars he'd sent to Bruce's offshore bank was nothing. He didn't care about the money. It was simply the point of it all. The man had not trusted Keeton because of his dual nature. And he'd lost his life as a result.

"We need to stick to this route, Bruce," he growled at the human who'd become increasingly toxic to their two-man operation.

"Think I'm gonna trust a fucking animal. I'll go this way," the man argued.

After a few more minutes of trying to convince him, Keeton threw his hands up. His beast scratched at his skin, the animal sensing something was not right. The sounds of the explosion and Bruce's bitter cry rang in his ears, but he died before Keeton could ever hope to reach him.

It was his fault. He was the reason Bruce had died. After pledging his life to help save lives, he'd brought death instead.

Keeton was better off on his own.

Excerpt from Fangs For Nothin'
by C.D. Gorri

"Are you out of your mind?"

Xavier DuMont, Vampire and Prince of the Tenebris Clan out of DuMont, New Jersey, ran a hand over his face. It was almost five in the morning on Wednesday, and he was still going over the weekly requests and complaints.

He could not believe it. One after the other, he'd received dozens of requests for formal introductions for most of the eligible young females in the Clan by their parents or some family matchmaker or other. It was the 21st Century, and yet, the Vampires of the Tenebris Clan still thought he needed an arranged marriage to run things!

"No, Lucius, I assure you my mind is sound."

"How can you be thinking of going away? To some retreat? At this time of year! You know, the whole Clan is up in arms over the tax laws your father had set into motion before his demise. Some are questioning your right to rule. Then, there is still the matter of your mating—"

"Lucius, for the love of fuck! I know what is going on in my own Clan. I am even now revoking those tax laws, people will just have to be patient."

"And what about meeting with these young females? Maybe that will quell some of the unrest—"

"No! I am not inclined to take a mate at this time. My father's grave has barely begun to grow grass. There is no rush!"

"There is pressure though, sire," Lucius Redwing insisted.

He was Xavier's oldest and most reliable friend. At nearly three hundred years old, they'd known each other for a considerable length of time. Lucius had been his childhood companion when they'd fled France for the New World. After settling the town of DuMont, his father had not only been the most productive of the local normals, but he had taken over their branch of the Clan.

Breaking ties with the old regime, and establishing their own rule, the DuMonts had done exceedingly well. Of course, coming into the new century had been difficult for some, but Xavier was determined to do it, to breathe new life into the old-fashioned world of Vampires. He would see them succeed and blossom in this age that was simply exploding with technology.

"I know you have plans, sire. But the anxious mamas are already parading their daughters resumes as if they were applying for a job." Lucius grinned. He waved a manila envelope bursting with applications for audiences with him from the most prestigious Vampire families in all of DuMont.

"For fuck's sake, Luc. Get rid of them," Xavier growled, and ran a hand over his face.

"Now, now. Surely, you know enough not to disrespect tradition and courtesy. These families are your staunchest supporters. Without their aid, your ascension to leadership could be challenged. The right mate would stop all of that—"

"I will not be forced into this, Luc. If anyone wants to challenge me for the right to lead, then he or she can face me out in the open. Not hide behind some political game."

"But sire—"

"No. I will not be manipulated. You should know that of me, old friend."

"Yes. Of course." Lucius nodded, placing the hefty envelope on the corner of Xavier's desk.

Vampires did not always inherit the right to lead. Princes were not born but made. Wasn't that what his father had always said? And yet, royal blood flowed in his veins. And it was because of that blood —*his royal DuMont blood*—that so many hungry mamas yearned to tie one of their young to him for eternity.

Fortunately, Xavier had avoided them. He refused to be pressured to take any of the hungry misses for his mate, as of yet. But with his recent ascension, that pressure was now on full keel.

Shit and fuck.

"I've got an idea," Lucius said, thrusting a copy of *The Nightly News* at him.

"What is it, Luc? I am in no mood."

"Read there," his friend said, pointing at an article on the bottom left.

"A retreat? I haven't been on one of those since I was ninety."

"Yes, but remember the fun? I brought my *sheep* at the time, and you pouted because I wouldn't share her!"

"As I recall, she came quite willingly to my bed when summoned, Luc. Why do they still call them sheep? My gods, that is positively medieval!" he replied.

"In case normals see the newspaper, of course."

"Impossible. The Covens bespelled the paper to only go to supes."

"It has happened, Xavier. You know this as well as I."

"True. And Luc, I am sorry about Temple. That was your donor at the time, was it not?"

"Temple? Yes. Not to worry, sire. You always did woo the ladies without trying. Besides, now they have their own donors on hand. You do not need to bring one."

"You don't have to do that, you know."

"What?"

"Calling me sire."

"I do have to call you sire, *sire*. You are my Prince."

"Oh, do shut up. I am your friend, Luc. You've known me my entire life."

"Yes, sire."

"Luc," he growled his friend's name.

"Shall I make the arrangements then?"

"Fine. I will go to this retreat for the weekend if

only to shut you up. And to get away from all this." He indicated the pile of correspondence.

"Very good, sire."

Excerpt from The Enforcer by C.D. Gorri

The moon would soon be full. Isabeau looked at the night sky and pulled the hood of her ivory sweater up over her fiery red curls. She passed between the red and sugar maples, a few tall beech trees, and a lonely pine when a low growl sounded next to her. She reached out to touch the thick fur of the adult she-Wolf who walked beside her through the forest trail.

"It's okay Artemis, let's finish our rounds and get home."

As she walked around the perimeter of her land she chanted an ancient language that few would be able to identify fortifying the wards around her large animal sanctuary. That was what the mortals around her thought it was, and for the most part they were correct.

To them, Isabeau Rose had just arrived in town a few years ago with the deed to five-hundred acres of Northern New Jersey farmland. Within a few months, she'd transformed the abandoned horse farm and the woods around it into a series of habitats for wild animals that were injured or discarded. Creatures that needed a haven for rehabilitation.

She had a main house for herself that boasted ten-bedrooms and six-full baths, an indoor pool and spa, two stables, one for her horses, the other for more exotic wildlife, two large red barns, and a state of the art veterinary clinic on the grounds.

"Out late, aren't you?" Beau turned around to find the source of the unfamiliar voice. She lifted her hand to calm Artemis who was ready to pounce on the intruder.

"Who are you?" she demanded.

"The real question is what are you doing out here so late? Surely your wards don't need reinforcement at this time of night, not out in this quiet New Jersey forest, Sorceress Rose?" The dark stranger spoke with an unearthly calm to his voice that put Beau on edge.

This was no mere mortal. She used her keen

sight to see him despite the darkness and almost gasped aloud. His face was perfect, except for a thin silver scar that ran from his left eyebrow to his chin. His eyes blazed cerulean blue fringed with impossibly dark lashes. They were carefully masked to hide his emotions.

About the Author

C.D. Gorri is a USA Today Bestselling author of steamy paranormal romance and urban fantasy. She is the creator of the Grazi Kelly Universe.

Join her mailing list here: https://www.cdgorri.com/newsletter

An avid reader with a profound love for books and literature, when she is not writing or taking care of her family, she can usually be found with a book or tablet in hand. C.D. lives in her home state of New Jersey where many of her characters or stories are based. Her tales are fast paced yet detailed with satisfying conclusions.

If you enjoy powerful heroines and loyal heroes who face relatable problems in supernatural settings, journey into the Grazi Kelly Universe today. You will find sassy, curvy heroines and sexy, love-driven heroes who find their HEAs between the pages. Werewolves, Bears, Dragons, Tigers, Witches, Romani, Lynxes, Foxes, Thunderbirds, Vampires, and many more Shifters and supernatural creatures dwell within her worlds. The most important thing is every mate in this universe is fated, loyal, and true lovers always get their happily ever afters.

Want to know how it all began? Enter the Grazi Kelly Universe with Wolf Moon: A Grazi Kelly Novel or pick up Charley's Christmas Wolf and dive into the Macconwood Pack Novel Series today.

For a complete list of C.D. Gorri's books visit her website here:

https://www.cdgorri.com/complete-book-list/

Thank you and happy reading!

del mare alla stella,
    C.D. Gorri

Follow C.D. Gorri here:
    http://www.cdgorri.com
    https://www.facebook.com/Cdgorribooks

https://www.bookbub.com/authors/c-d-gorri

https://twitter.com/cgor22

https://instagram.com/cdgorri/

https://www.goodreads.com/cdgorri

https://www.tiktok.com/@cdgorriauthor